Fatality at the Fair

Fatality at the Fair

A Finch & Fischer Mystery

J New

Fatality at the Fair
A Finch & Fischer Mystery
Book 4

Copyright © J. New 2022

The right of J. New to be identified as the author of this work has been asserted in accordance with the Copyright, Designs and Patents Act 1988. All rights reserved. No part of this publication may be reproduced, stored in or transmitted into any retrieval system, in any form, or by any means (electronic, mechanical, photocopying, recording or otherwise) without the prior written permission of the publisher. Any person who does any unauthorised act in relation to this publication may be liable to criminal prosecution and civil claims for damages.

This is a work of fiction. Names, characters, businesses, places, events and incidents are either the products of the author's imagination or used in a fictitious manner. Any resemblance to actual persons, living or dead, or actual events is purely coincidental.

Cover design copyright © J. New
Cover design by J. New
Interior formatting by Alt 19 Creative

OTHER BOOKS BY J. NEW

The Yellow Cottage Vintage Mysteries in order:
The Yellow Cottage Mystery (Free.
See back of book for details)
An Accidental Murder
The Curse of Arundel Hall
A Clerical Error
The Riviera Affair
A Double Life

The Finch & Fischer Mysteries in order:
Decked in the Hall
Death at the Duck Pond
Battered to Death
Fatality at the Fair

Tea & Sympathy Mysteries in order:
Tea & Sympathy
A Deadly Solution
Tiffin & Tragedy
A Bitter Bouquet
A Frosty Combination
Steeped in Murder
Storm in a Teacup
High Tea Low Opinions

ONE

The weekend of the Queen's birthday was the perfect excuse for the village of Hambleton Chase to throw a good celebration party. An annual event and the highlight of the summer for the whole of Hantchester county, it had started years ago when Penny was still in school. Or 'knee high to a grasshopper,' as her father always said. It was the one weekend that Penny, along with almost everyone else in the area, looked forward to the most.

It was an open invitation to all the residents of the six villages and hamlets that made up Hampsworthy Downs, as well as those from both Winstoke and the larger towns beyond. It had become so popular over the years that there was also a huge influx of tourists who marked it in the calendar every year, and arrived toting a variety of suitcases, pets and children and filled up every hotel, guest house bed-and-breakfast and campsite within a five-mile radius. It would take an army of Buckingham Palace guards to keep them away, and even then there would be no guarantee of success.

The weather was warm and sunny, but even if it had been raining, it wouldn't have dampened the spirits of the locals when it came to celebrating the birth of their beloved monarch. Many of the older residents, when they were children, remembered vividly watching the coronation in 1953 on their small black and white televisions sets, nearly all of which had been purchased purely to see the event. It was the first time the coronation of a British monarch had been televised, and everyone wanted to be a part of it. In total, 27 million people in the UK watched the ceremony on television, with a further 11 million tuning in and listening via radio. To them, Queen Elizabeth was practically part of the family.

Penny pulled the door to her cottage closed and locked it, pocketing the key. At her heel was her best friend and partner in crime, Fischer. He was an adorable, loving and very clever Jack Russell Terrier who Penny had rescued as a puppy, and he'd stolen her heart from the moment she'd found him.

"Ready, little man?" Penny asked, looking down at her diminutive pal.

Fischer met her gaze, tongue lolling from the side of his grinning mouth and a look of pure love in his brown eyes. He was wearing a bright royal blue bow tie and looked very smart and extremely excited. Impatient to be off. He somehow knew this extra adornment meant he was visiting somewhere special.

Penny clipped the red, white, and blue lead to his harness and opened the gate. The village of Cherrytree Downs was adorned with red, white and blue bunting fluttering in the gentle morning breeze. Flags were hanging from windows and doors and balloons were tied to various gates. Some of the older residents had even knitted special toppers for the red post boxes. Penny smiled as she passed one of the Queen herself, wearing her crown and with a corgi at her side. It was absolutely amazing. She stopped to take a picture with her phone.

The warm air carried the sounds of happy chatter as families from all over the village congregated at the bus stop by the village green. Awaiting the transport that would take them to the large sports field where the fair and the celebrations would take place.

As soon as she arrived and joined the queue, Fischer became the centre of attention as the children flocked to see him. He entertained them with his repertoire of tricks, which delighted child and adult alike.

As the only mobile librarian serving the area, Penny knew just about everyone, and as Fischer was always at her side, they all knew him, too. In fact, she had it on good authority that several of the locals looked forward to the weekly visit from the library purely because it gave them a chance to make a fuss of the little dog. He was perfect therapy for those living alone.

At the same time as she heard the sound of the approaching bus, Penny saw her mum and dad, Albert and Sheila Finch, sauntering up the lane arm-in-arm.

"Just in time," Penny said, giving her parents' a quick hug each. "Although I'm sure old Fred would have waited for you."

"Morning, love," Sheila said, bending down to greet Fischer. "And how is my star pupil today?"

Fischer woofed and grinned, his tail whirring enthusiastically.

"He's very proud of his bow tie," Penny said with an indulgent smile. "Do you think it will help him win the dog show?"

"Oh, I've no doubt it will help. He looks splendid. But it will be our clever tricks that get us the prize. Isn't that right, Fischer?"

In response to the question, and a quick signal from Sheila, Fischer lay down, rolled over once, then ended in a sitting position, one paw raised for a hand-shake. Albert did the honours. The queue of people broke into spontaneous applause and Sheila smiled, reached into her pocket and gave Fischer a well-earned treat.

"Penny! Fischer!" two excited voices shouted from behind.

Penny turned and found Billy and Ellen Hughes running towards them. They were the children of her best friend and local reporter, Susie.

"Good morning, you two. Where's your mum?"

"She's coming," Billy replied, giving Fischer a hug.

"All aboard the Ups and Downs," Fred called out from the bus. "Next stop the fair."

Penny saw Susie speed walking up the lane, eventually arriving out of breath and clutching her side.

"Just in time. You look worn out all ready, Susie."

"It's always a last minute rush with the kids in a morning. Billy lost one of his trainers and Ellen decided at the last minute she wanted to change her outfit."

Penny laughed.

"Come on. You can rest on the bus."

"Thank goodness for that. I've got an awful stitch. I'm too old for this rushing about at the last minute lark."

The old bus was a classic, over sixty-five years old and running as though it had just rolled off the production line that very morning. She was a PS1 Tiger single decker with a Barnaby coachwork, now a rare collector's item and famous around the downs. In bright green and cream with a red flash, she turned heads whenever she was brought out for special occasions.

Inside, the brown leather and chrome steel framed seats were almost full. Penny and Susie found two across the narrow aisle from one another and stowed their bags on the string mesh luggage rack above their heads. Today it was strung with Union Jack bunting. Fischer jumped onto Penny's lap and made himself comfortable. With a final toot of the horn, Fred pulled out to the cheers of the passengers.

Five minutes into the journey, as Fred left the village behind, the passengers started opening Tupperware boxes and sharing the contents. Soon the bus was filled with the tantalising sweet smells of sweets and pastries.

Albert Finch leaned into the aisle from behind his daughter and shook a tartan flask in her and Susie's direction.

"Either of you want some tea?"

"Ooo, yes please, Mr Finch. I could do with a cuppa," Susie said, taking the proffered cup and trying to hold it steady as Fred bumped over the road and Albert poured. He did the same for Penny, and soon they were sipping a very good cup of English breakfast tea.

At the next stop in Rowan Downs, the passengers were joined by several more excited children and their parents. Now every seat was spoken for and Fred couldn't take anymore on board.

"Don't worry, Old Shirley is right behind me," he told those waiting in line on the pavement.

Penny saw her friend Mr Kelly waiting patiently and waved.

"I'll see you there," she mouthed through the window, and Mr Kelly smiled and gave her a thumbs up. Then pointed behind. Old Shirley was just coming up the road.

Fred indicated and pulled out. Soon they were leaving Rowan Downs, and ignoring the junction to Winstoke, passed Chips Ahoy, which was also covered in the Union Flag bunting. The building had been given a face-lift recently and looked bright, cheerful and welcoming. But Penny couldn't help but shudder when she thought about what had happened there a few months previously.

Suddenly she felt a cold, wet nose on her cheek. Swiftly followed by a quick lick. She gave Fischer a kiss on his head. He always sensed when she was concerned about something.

"I'm fine, Fish Face. Don't worry. I'm always fine with you around."

As the last vestiges of the village gave way to fields and hedgerows, Penny saw someone had planted little flags all along the grass verges, and in the field a creative farmer had dressed the scarecrow as the Queen herself, with a crown on her head and waving a flag.

Albert Finch leaned forward.

"Remember when you were a little girl, and you swore you hadn't been crawling through the hedgerows in the village?"

Penny laughed.

"I can't believe I thought I'd get away with it, considering my knees were covered in mud and grass stains. I used to hide in there to read my books."

"I had a devil of a job trying to get those stains out," her mum added. "You ruined many a pair of good school tights crawling through those hedgerows. And you did too, Susie."

"Believe me, Mrs Finch, I have every empathy. Now I'm a mother myself."

The old hedges were ancient boundaries around the villages and farmland of Hampsworthy Downs. They had grown into thick wildlife habitats. At various points in the village she had grown up in, it had been possible for Penny to enter and crawl along the hidden green tunnels for what seemed like miles. It was a magical space, and she had no doubt they still existed and were used by the current generation of children for their dens and secret club headquarters.

At the next village, Fred drove straight through, tooting his horn at those waiting at the bus stop. The second bus, with Shirley at the wheel, slowed to a stop to pick them all up.

Eventually Fred pulled into the sports field at Hambleton chase and parked. Penny could see the place was already packed with people milling about the stalls and fair rides.

She grinned at Susie, who grinned back. It was like being a kid again. Both of them were thinking back to what they'd got up to as teenagers at the fair in years gone by.

They were really looking forward to the festivities.

With Billy and Ellen racing on ahead, Susie and Penny walked with Penny's parents through the gate into the main field. Every so often Billy and Ellen would charge back and grab their mother's hand, pulling her along with cries of, "Come on, Mum."

Susie rolled her eyes.

"Looks like my first stop is the fairground. I'll catch up with you all later."

"And I want to go and have a look at the agility course Fischer will be using," Sheila said. "Although, I'm sure we can do it all with no problems. Isn't that right, little man?" She bent down to give the smiling dog a head scratch.

"I'll walk that far with you," Albert said. "Then I'll go and have a look at the display on the far side of the field. They have all the old tractors and farm equipment from donkey's years ago. Some of it's even for sale."

"Don't you dare come home having bought a tractor, Albert Finch," Sheila said with mock severity.

"Of course not, dear. What would I do with a tractor? I've got my eye on a combine harvester. What about you, Penny? Where are you headed first?"

"I've no destination in mind, dad. I'll just wander around and see what takes my fancy."

There was a loud crackle followed by a buzz and a brief high-pitched squeal as the Tannoy system sprang into life, and the voice of Ted, the compere, rang out through the surrounding speakers welcoming them all to the annual fair to celebrate the birth of their Monarch. The first verse and chorus of God Save the Queen was played, with everyone standing and joining in, then Ted got down to the announcements. As he read from the order of events, Penny said goodbye to her mum and dad, then started to stroll the perimeter with an eager Fischer.

In the centre of the field was a large circle display area. Cordoned off with tape and surrounded by large stacked bales of hay intended for seating. This would be where the dog agility would be set up, but for now there was a bird of prey demonstration just starting. Fischer was fascinated, so Penny let him watch the magnificent birds fly from one side to the other, landing on the gloves of their trainers and being rewarded with chunks of meat.

Further along, more tape marked out the race tracks for the egg and spoon, sack, and three-legged races. Penny sauntered to the edge of the field nearest the entrance where fast food vendors had pitched a variety of tents, wooden chalets and vehicles selling everything from old-fashioned sweets, pancakes, pizza and paella. To pastries, cakes, soups and salads. There was even a sushi stall. All of this was alongside the more traditional offerings of hot dogs, burgers and fish and chips. Penny was also very pleased to see a couple of vegan and vegetarian vendors in amongst it all, and made a mental note to come back when she was ready to eat.

At the far end, a huge marquee had been erected. This was the craft tent where local artisans had set out their wares to sell. Wooden toys, glassware, jewellery, garden ornaments and macramé items, mixed with larger items such as up-cycled furniture and paintings.

Penny caught the heavy scent of pot-pourri mixed with patchouli and was drawn to the tent entrance like the Bisto kid in one of the old adverts. Fischer gave a sudden sneeze and shook his head. Then wagged his tail and followed Penny.

Inside, the noisy hubbub of the fair was muffled by the heavy white canvas. Neat lines of tables were adorned with wonderful, brightly coloured displays. Every item charming and attractive in its own right. Penny knew she had to exercise enormous restraint if she was to stop herself from buying one of everything. A small silver dragon ornament caught her eye, and she drifted towards it. Then she spotted the teapots.

All handmade and hand-painted, the display was stunning. Just about every possible shape and design was represented. From the traditional and classic to more adventurous ones like an elephant. There was even one shaped like a hot-air balloon, and another like a cauliflower. Penny spent ages studying them. Lifting them up to test their weights, removing lids and peering inside, before carefully replacing them with a satisfying clink. She smiled at the stall holder, who she could see was almost sure Penny was going to buy something.

"These are all so beautiful it's difficult to choose. I'll come back later," she said, forcing herself to step away. "I'll need to think about how much space I have at home."

Penny's teapot collection was still growing, and while she wasn't going to deprive herself of a new one, she knew there was only so much room left. Whatever she chose needed to be practical as well as beautiful, because all her teapots were used.

She left the craft tent through the exit at the opposite end so deep in thought about whether she should buy the cauliflower one, the hot-air balloon, or really push the boat out and splurge on both, she very nearly walked straight into a wall of hay bales. It was almost six feet high and ran from the boundary hedge straight across into the field itself. She followed it and at the end discovered it opened out into an archery range.

Tony Deacon was at the opening making safe the long arrows by stabbing them into a bale of hay. There was also a collection of short bows in a wooden trunk by his feet.

"Penny Finch," he said. "Fancy giving it a go?" He picked up a bow and offered it to her.

"I'm not sure, Tony. I've never done it before. I'd hate for it to go wild and hurt someone."

Deacon waved his arm expansively to indicate the two walls of hay bales on either side of the range, as well as another at the far end directly behind the target.

"All health and safety concerns have been addressed. There's no need to worry about an accident."

He picked up a bow.

"And these bows are very safe."

He notched one of the longer arrows and, taking aim, let it fly straight down the range where it hit the target dead centre.

Penny smiled.

"Well done. I'm impressed. Maybe I will try later. Thanks, Tony."

Penny left the archery range with Fischer happily trotting at her side and walked around the perimeter to the food marquee pitched at the bottom of the bale safety wall, about thirty yards to one side of the target. It had been set up against the edge of the field with its back along the hedgerow. She glanced back and over the stack of hay and could see Tony Deacon had once again notched an arrow in readiness.

"Well, at least he's getting in some practice," Penny said to her little dog, just as raised voices from the food tent reached her ears. She frowned. Now what's this all about?

TWO

Janet Cotton suddenly stormed out of the food tent.

"No, Derek," she shouted over her shoulder. "I'm not spending the day cooped up in that tent with you."

She stopped and turned on her heel as Derek Cotton followed her out. She took a step towards him, finger jabbing in his face.

"The sooner you let me go, the better it will be for both of us," she hissed.

She saw Penny watching and her face flushed an angry red. With nothing more to say, she marched away. Obviously angry.

"Till death do us part, my dear," Derek called out to her retreating back, in bitter and sarcastic tones.

"And you'd know all about death, wouldn't you?" she retorted.

Penny didn't know where to look. She glanced at Fischer, who had sat down, but was leaning against her leg. He didn't like confrontation. She reached down and stroked his neck, letting him know it was all right. When she rose, she saw Tony Deacon was watching. He was gripping a bow, his knuckles white with the effort. But he wasn't interested in her. He was glaring at Derek Cotton who was returning to the food tent. A snarl on his lip. He spun round and quickly, notching another arrow, let it loose. It hit the target at the end with a loud thump.

"Come on, Fish Face, let's see if we can find ourselves a tasty treat inside."

The tent was filled with a heady miasma of glorious scents, but the atmosphere was still frosty after the argument between the Cottons. Penny and Fischer ambled down the tables, perusing everything on offer and sampling an assortment of homemade vegetarian pies, pastries, pickles and jams, and far too many sweet treats.

Alan Dubois, the restaurant critic, was standing in front of a cake stall where small samples on paper doilies were set out. Everything from fruit cake to Victoria sponge. Dubois, after some careful thought, selected one and popped it into his mouth. He ate with his eyes closed, presumably to savour the taste, Penny thought. Then, after cleaning his palate with a mouthful of water from the cup in his hand, and dabbing the corners of his mouth with a white handkerchief, he tried another and repeated the exercise. Penny smiled to herself. It all seemed a bit pretentious to her.

She recognised the amateur baker. It was Amanda, the receptionist from The Rough Spot, the veterinary practice in Cherrytree Downs. Fischer had also identified her, and with a little whine, positioned himself behind her legs. Penny picked him up and gave him a cuddle. The last time she'd taken Fischer to the vets, Amanda had held him still while the vet had given him a vaccination, as the regular nurse was busy with another customer. It seemed Fischer remembered the occasion vividly.

"It's okay, Fischer, we're not here to see Amanda. She's not even noticed us. She's too busy with the food critic, look."

The receptionist's attention was wholly focused on Alan. She looked nervous, head tilted to one side while she awaited his opinion. He opened his eyes and looked at her briefly before breaking out into a broad smile. She beamed, clearly delighted.

Dubois moved to the next table. It belonged to Derek Cotton. His stand had a banner set up advertising 'Bistro 23.' It was the name of his restaurant in Winstoke on Market Street.

"Keep walking, Dubois," Derek growled. "I'm not wasting my samples on the likes of you."

Penny was surprised at his tone. Obviously, he was still upset about the altercation with his wife, but surely there was no need to take it out on somebody else?

Alan Dubois showed no signs of being bothered by the rebuke and casually walked on, ignoring Derek Cotton completely. But Derek hadn't finished.

"You've had your last bite from me. That review you did for my bistro will be the last bad review you ever do. When I've finished dragging you through the courts, you'll be bankrupt. You'll be eating scraps out of bins by the time I've finished with you."

"You will not antagonise me, Mr Cotton," Alan Dubois said nonchalantly.

"Antagonise? Antagonise!" Cotton shouted. "I'll antagonise you on the sports field if you're not careful."

While Derek obviously didn't know the meaning of the word antagonise, his intention was clear. Amanda tried to calm him down, but to no avail. His mood and anger was putting a bad taste in everyone's mouth.

Alan moved to the next table where Linda Green was setting out her homemade jams, cakes and bread. She glared at Derek.

"They aren't even your recipes, Derek. They're mine. You stole them from me. It ought to be me who sues you."

"Rubbish. These are my recipes," Derek said. "Call yourself a cook? You couldn't make a decent sandwich."

Linda stopped what she was doing and marched to Cotton's table. She snatched a sample and took a bite. Immediately, she wrinkled her nose, grabbed a serviette, and coughed the contents out. She dropped the whole lot into a nearby bin.

"You can't even get it right. First you steal my recipes, then you murder them."

Dubois lingered at Linda's stall without sampling anything. Penny noticed he was standing with his back to the argument. He carefully dabbed his mouth with his white handkerchief and glanced over his shoulder at Derek Cotton. His eyes narrowing.

Penny was beginning to feel flushed and awkward. She needed to get away from the awful atmosphere in the food tent and back to the happiness outside.

Still carrying Fischer, she exited and, putting her four legged pal back on the ground, walked away. Breathing in the fresh, sunny air, she immediately felt better.

———•———

Fischer tugged her toward the perimeter hedge and while she waited for him to finish his business, she filled his water bowl. Walking back behind the hay bale wall, she saw her friend Mr Kelly watching some youngsters try their hand at archery.

"Penny," Mr Kelly said brightly as he spotted her. "And hello little, Fischer. Did you know there was a time when it was every man's duty to practice their archery skills should the king ever call them to battle? The Archery Law of 1252 required all lower-class males of fighting age be capable of using a bow and arrow. Weekly target practice was compulsory, and the law stated every village had to have a designated area to practice. Amusingly, it was called a butt."

Penny grinned as some of the children started giggling.

"I didn't know that, Mr Kelly. It's very interesting."

They watched as a young boy launched his arrow. It flew halfway down the range before thudding into the turf.

"It's too far," the boy complained.

"Nonsense. It's only twenty yards. Shorter than a cricket wicket. I bet you could throw a cricket ball that far and take out the middle stump," Tony Deacon said.

A father stood over his boy and started to wipe clean a bow.

"You might make a better shot if these bows weren't covered in ice-cream. Too many sticky hands have been on these bows already."

Tony Deacon took offense at the man's words.

"I've got enough to do making sure these kids don't shoot anywhere but down the range and collecting the arrows after they've been fired."

"Launched," Mr Kelly said, correcting him.

Deacon stopped and stared at Mr Kelly.

"You can't fire an arrow. It's not a firearm. You launch an arrow. Shoot it maybe, but certainly not fire."

"We're not in school now, sir," Deacon replied in a patronising tone.

"It's never too late to learn," Mr Kelly said, unperturbed by Deacon's sarcasm. "Especially when there are young minds around."

Deacon was still scowling as Penny led her friend away.

"Do you know him, Mr Kelly?" Penny asked once they were out of earshot. "Did you teach him?"

Mr Kelly shook his head.

"I never taught him, but I do know him. He was a local teacher. Now a youth activities coordinator for Hantchester County."

"A teacher?" Penny said, surprised. "He doesn't look as though he likes children very much."

"He was always good at crowd control. But I'm not sure how much the children actually learned from him. He was a bit of a shouter, so I heard. But he left the profession after a particular incident. He lost his temper in the staff room one day. Lashed out at the staff mugs of all things, and dashed them all to the floor in a fit of pique, apparently. He has a bit of a temper."

"Better lashing out at the crockery than the staff or the pupils," Penny said.

"Oh, indeed."

Penny took another glance at Tony Deacon, seeing him in a different light. He was walking towards the target, gathering up arrows in readiness for the next practice round.

"I'm on my way to the garden produce display," Mr Kelly said. "My daughter has entered her flower arrangements this year and is hoping for a medal."

Penny and Fischer walked along with him for a short distance, but then Penny spied Billy and Ellen racing towards her, giggling and laughing. Behind them, hurrying to keep up without breaking into a run, was Susie.

"I'll find you later, Mr Kelly. Give my best wishes and lots of luck to Laura."

"Penny. Penny. Penny." The children jumped up and down at her feet, fussing with Fischer, and told her all the things they had seen and done so far. Penny managed to take the somewhat garbled information in, overwhelmed by their enthusiasm for every little thing.

"I've been round the entire field already, but hardly seen a thing," Susie said breathlessly. "They just want to race from one thing to the next."

"Ice cream. Ice cream," the kids began to chant, seeing the van.

"I'll get those," Penny said, pulling a five pound note from her purse and handing it to Susie. "They can share the change."

Susie held up her hand to refuse.

"I can afford them, you know. I don't have to pinch the pennies quite as much as I used to."

"I know. I just want to treat them."

Susie acquiesced.

"All right, but I'm treating you to lunch at the Pot and Kettle next time. Agreed?"

Penny rolled her eyes and smiled. She knew wouldn't win that argument with her best friend, so nodded and accepted her offer. Then Susie was off again, running to keep up with her hyper active children. She was watching them stand on tiptoes to point at various pictures of lollies and cones when a scream cut across the warm dry air. Penny whirled round to see where it came from. One of the more frightening rides over at the fairground had reached the top and was just plunging down. A group of girls were screaming in joyful terror.

"Phew," Penny said to Fischer. "I thought something awful had happened for a minute."

As a cloud rolled momentarily over the sun, casting a long shadow which raced away over Sugar Hill to the South West, the tannoy once again crackled to life and Ted announced the next events. The sack race, three legged, and egg and spoon races were due to start in ten minutes. Penny had wondered if she and Susie should enter this year, it had been a long time since the two of them had last lost their footing in the three-legged race, tumbling to the floor just short of the finish line, totally helpless with laughter.

She wandered in the direction of the racetrack. White lines marking the lanes and a tape fence holding back spectators. There was already a small crowd gathering, but head and shoulders above the rest, Penny saw DI John Monroe and her stomach gave an involuntary flip. She raised her hand in a wave, but his eyes seemed to pass over her.

"Come on, Fish Face, let's go and say hello."

He was wearing a white shirt with no tie and the top buttons undone. Smart trousers and polished shoes. He held his jacket over one shoulder with his index finger, while the other hand was in his trouser pocket. He looked more smart than casual, so could very well be on duty, she thought, hoping she was wrong. It would be nice to wander around the fair and see all the sights with him.

"Hello, John," she said, as Fischer bounded over and jumped up for a pat. "I didn't think I would see you here."

"Hello, Penny. Hello Fischer." He bent down to scratch the dog's chin, then faced Penny. "It's the only thing anyone has been talking about at the station this week. So I thought I'd better come and experience it for myself. It seems the whole of the county and beyond have turned up. I didn't expect it to be this busy."

"It's the highlight of the year. Although I must say it seems busier this year than I ever remember it. No wonder you didn't see me waving."

"Did you wave?" Monroe asked. "I am sorry. My vision is a bit blurry at the moment. A spot of hay fever, unfortunately. Must be all the freshly cut grass. I've taken a tablet and put in some drops, so it should go off soon."

They fell into step as they walked through the crowds. The smell of grass and toffee apples, candy floss and donuts filling the air with warm sugary scents.

"It's nice to bump into you," Penny said. "I haven't seen you for a while."

"It's taken a lot longer to set up the office in Winstoke than I anticipated. But we're running like a well-oiled machine now. I've got to know my team well. They're a good bunch of officers. It's a pleasure working with them all. Hopefully I'll get a bit more free time in the future. Well, Sundays off at least."

The pair stopped and turned to one another, but whatever might have happened was ruined by a priggish voice calling their names.

"Pens. Johnny."

Penny froze as a cold shiver shiver ran down her spine and felt Fischer pull away. When he realised Penny wasn't moving, he sat by her feet, his back to the owner of the voice. It was Edward, Penny's former fiancé.

"Edward," Monroe said.

"What's she bending your ear about now, John? Someone late with their library book?" he sucked at his teeth. "Better get the constabulary on it, Pens. No doubt on the run, fearful of the seventy-five pence fine you're going to slap them with."

Edward burst out laughing at this very tired and very weak joke at Penny's expense. She just stared at him. Embarrassed for him rather than for herself.

"I'm sure Penny is more than capable of taking care of her own business without calling in the detectives, Ed. She's practically an honorary detective herself," John replied, cool and polite.

Penny had to stop herself from grinning at the put down. Not only had John called Edward Ed, which he hated, but he'd really buoyed up her own reputation. She and Fischer had been extremely helpful in three previous cases of suspicious death. Then John's phone rang. He stepped aside and took the call. A moment later, he hung up.

"I'm sorry, Penny, I have to go. Duty calls. Hopefully, I'll bump into you again shortly. Goodbye, Edward."

"Never a day off with that one," Edward said. "Far too serious."

Penny didn't expect Edward to have anything nice to say about John Monroe, or anyone, for that matter. But maybe he was just a little jealous seeing her and the handsome Detective Inspector together. Perhaps it had made him think about what he'd lost when he had an affair with a work colleague. Penny was actually glad it had happened in hindsight. She was much better off and far, far happier without him. She was spared the ordeal of having to make small talk when her mother appeared. She turned to say goodbye to Edward, but he'd already wandered off without a word. Probably scared off by Sheila.

"Penny. There you are. I've been looking all over for you. I've come to collect my little star. It's time for the dog competition."

Fischer jumped up excitedly, barking and spinning in circles.

"See, he already knows it's time," Sheila said, taking his lead.

"Good luck, mum. Good luck, Fish Face. I'll be cheering you on."

Penny wandered around the large central display area until she found the man she was looking for perched on a hay bale, holding a plastic glass of beer. He'd got the best seat in the house.

"Hi, dad," she said, giving him a quick peck on the cheek.

"Want to share my bale?" Albert Finch said, shifting up a bit to make room.

"How do you think he'll do?" Penny asked once she was comfortably installed next to her dad.

"Fischer? Heavens, need you ask? He's the firm favourite. The smartest one in the ring by a country mile."

Penny laughed.

"Do you think you're a bit biased, dad?"

"Of course. But I'm still right. There's no one on either four legs or two who can touch him. Oh look, it's starting."

The obedience display came first, followed by simple tricks. Sheila Finch took Fischer through his paces and he didn't put a single paw wrong. He performed every one of his tricks to perfection, his blue bow tie bouncing as he went through his well rehearsed routine. There was tremendous applause after he'd stood on his hind legs and walked backwards.

"Wow," Penny said, wide eyed and open-mouthed. "I didn't know he could do that. Isn't he brilliant!"

"Wait for the next one," Albert said, who'd been watching his wife train Fischer for months.

Sheila walked forward using wide strides while Fischer weaved in and out of her legs continually, never missing a beat.

Penny was entranced. She stood up, clapping her little dog on. So proud of what he could do.

"Fischer's doing really well," someone said.

Penny turned and found Amanda, the vet receptionist, beside her.

"Hi, Amanda. Isn't he? I can't believe how much he's learned. Mum has really worked hard with him and you can tell he's enjoying every minute of it. So, who's looking after your cake stall while you're taking a break?"

Amanda waved her hand. "It's fine. It's very quiet in there at the moment. No customers, only arguing chefs, and quite frankly, I'd had enough of all the posturing and testosterone flying about. It will get busy around lunch time, I would think. In any case, I wouldn't miss Fischer in the dog show. He's our favourite patient."

With that particular round finished, the judges came and eliminated several contestants, although the dogs got a rosette and a treat each for taking part. That left Fischer and a few others moving on to the final stage. The agility course. On the way passed, Sheila grinned at them both and gave them a double thumbs up.

"Good boy, Fischer!" Penny called out. "You're doing brilliantly."

"I think we're going to win," Albert said, when Penny sat down again. "Fischer hasn't put a foot wrong."

As the human and canine contestants lined up for their turn at the course, Penny glanced across the field. Many of the crowd had gathered for the dog show, but to one side, Penny noticed Alan Dubois leaving the food tent. He was furtively looking right and left before slipping between the canvas and the boundary hedge.

A loud bang made Penny jump. It sounded like an explosion. It put one dog and her owner completely off their stride. But, after a bit of a confab among the judges, they were allowed to return to the beginning of the course and start again. Surprise and concern rippled over the crowd, but then they realised it was the civil war re-enactment society firing a musket.

The tannoy whistled and squealed and Ted's voice came over the speakers, apologising for the interruption. An overly enthusiastic member of the re-enactment had fired off a volley early.

"The re-enactment of the battle of Cherrytree Downs, fought on the site of the Pig and Whistle pub between the Roundheads and the Cavaliers, where you can still see the scars from the bullets on the pub's old stone walls to this day, will commence in fifteen minutes."

Penny and Albert grinned at Ted's convoluted speech, then settled back to watch Fischer. But as the hubbub died down, Fischer suddenly slipped his lead and shot away, leaving the display ring. Sheila called after him and began to run. Penny and Albert also jumped off their bale and set off in pursuit. Penny was calling Fischer as she ran, terrified he'd run through the hedge onto the main road and be hit by a car. He'd never done this before. Something must have frightened him, causing him to bolt.

Suddenly, she saw what Fischer was aiming for.

Lying face down in the short grass was the unmistakable figure of a man. Fischer was barking, calling for help. Penny got to his side and picked him up, holding him close. Her heart beat wildly in her chest. She looked at the prostrate figure, knowing there was nothing she could do. He was still. An arrow piercing the side of his neck.

THREE

Penny couldn't believe what she was seeing. The blood from the wound was slowly seeping across the collar of the victim's shirt and spreading over the shoulder and down one sleeve.

She was vaguely aware of her parents standing next to her, urging her to come away and leave it to the police, but she was frozen to the spot.

She glanced up and at the end of the archery range, she saw Tony Deacon come into view outside the hay bale safety wall, a bundle of arrows in his arms. At the food tent, she noticed Alan Dubois looking flustered and oddly contrite.

Then she heard a scream piercing enough to crack glass.

A young woman, seeing the body face down in the grass, screamed again, her hands flew to her face and her knees buckled.

Fischer wriggled in Penny's arms and barked again, loud

and sharp, and she heard her dad shout for someone to quickly call an ambulance.

She heard a soft, calm voice in her ear and she looked into the serious but kind and concerned face of John Monroe.

"Penny, I need you to move away so I can preserve the scene."

She put a wriggling Fischer back on the ground and John gently took her by the arm, leading her out of the way.

"Oh, John. He's..." she trailed off. Couldn't speak the words.

John nodded in response.

"Yes."

Suddenly, she was surrounded by her parents and Susie. Sheila clipped on Fischer's lead and her father guided her to the edge of a small group of onlookers, all eager to see what had happened. Two police constables were already busy erecting a cordon to keep them at bay.

"Don't let the children see, Susie," Penny said, grasping her friend's arm.

"It's all right. They're over at the far side of the field, watching the Punch and Judy show. The school teachers and parent volunteers are looking after them."

In the distance, Penny heard the sound of an approaching ambulance. In the warm summer air, the high-pitched wail of the siren carried for miles.

"Who is it?" Susie asked.

Penny felt stronger now she had her parents and Susie by her side.

"I think it's Derek Cotton," she replied. "I saw him in the food tent earlier. I recognised his shirt and hair."

The opening of the food tent was only a few yards away from the body and it was deathly quiet there. Most of the festival crowd were either still at the central show ring or waiting for the civil war re-enactment to start. News of the accident hadn't yet spread. Suddenly, a volley of musket fire crackled in the distance at the far side of the field, followed by rising plumes of smoke. The show had begun.

"How on earth could this have happened?" Sheila said.

Penny observed the archery range. It was around thirty yards from the opening of the food tent. She'd seen the arrows fly the full length and hit the target no more than twenty yards away. Tony Deacon was staring from the shooting line, a bundle of arrows at his side.

"It must have been a terrible accident," Susie concluded.

The sound of the siren grew louder as the ambulance neared, and a short while later it rumbled over the sports field. The still small crowd parted to let it through and almost before it stopped, two paramedics leaped out and approached the scene.

Penny saw John Monroe speak with them briefly before they tended to the victim with calm precision and professionalism. He was laid face-down on the stretcher and carried to the waiting ambulance, the arrow obvious to everyone nearby. Penny clearly saw Derek Cotton's dead, staring eye. His head turned sideways, his face a death mask of pain and surprise.

The rear doors of the vehicle were slammed shut, and the ambulance moved off. It was telling that the flashing lights, and the siren had both been switched off.

———— ● ————

Monroe had now begun to scour the scene where Derek Cotton's body had been found. Carefully making notes and taking additional photographs. He'd already taken a plethora of images while the body was in situ.

He was joined by two members of his team who'd just arrived in a police car and parked just beyond the food tent. After a lot of discussion and gesticulating, he looked up and met Penny's eyes. He gave last-minute instructions to his men, then began to walk in her direction.

"Mum, could you look after Fischer? I'll be back in a minute. I think DI Monroe wants a word."

She met him halfway.

"How are you feeling, Penny?"

"I'm all right. Can I help with anything?"

"Actually, most of my team are tied up, and I wondered if you'd go over to Ted and ask him to make an announcement? We're closing down this half of the field. I don't want anyone contaminating the site."

"Of course. What should he say?"

"The less the better," he said with a wry smile. Ted's loquaciousness had obviously made an impression on him, too. "Just that there's been an incident and consequently this half of the field will be off limits for the foreseeable future. Apologise for any inconvenience. That sort of thing."

"Yes, okay."

"Thanks, Penny."

"I noticed you've taken him away already. Was there no need for the medical examiner?"

Monroe shook his head.

"Not this time. Cause of death was blatantly obvious and we can pin-point the time pretty well from when he was seen last compared to when you found him. We now need to workout exactly what happened."

On her way over to the compere's tent, Susie fell in to step with Penny.

"You okay, Penny?" Susie said.

"A bit shocked, but I'm okay."

"What do you know about Derek Cotton?"

"Are you interviewing me for your article?"

"If you don't mind?"

Penny shook her head.

"Go on. Ask your questions."

Susie retrieved a notebook and pen from her handbag and waited for her friend to answer.

"I probably know as much as anyone else in the area. He was the owner and manager of Bistro 23 in town. Not really my sort of place. There are no vegetarian options for a start, and it wasn't the nicest looking place. A bit scruffy, actually. But I did hear the food was quite good. Although not recently. Something happened, I think, but can't remember what."

"I don't think I've ever been," Susie said.

"You're not missing anything."

They'd reached Ted and while she relayed Monroe's message, Susie was scribbling. As the tannoy sprung into life, they made the return journey.

"I knew Derek Cotton when we were younger," Penny continued as they walked. "He always seemed to be in a bad mood. I don't think I ever remember seeing him smiling or happy. Last summer he told me to leave his premises because I had Fischer with me."

"He did not!" Susie exclaimed indignantly.

Penny smiled at her friend's outrage.

"He did. And I was sitting at one of his outside tables, not inside. I'd only stopped for a quick cup of tea and Fischer was as good as gold, laying quietly underneath the table. No one even knew he was there. But Derek said he didn't want dogs at his tables. In fact, he didn't want them anywhere near his restaurant full stop."

Derek Cotton had grown up in Cherrytree Downs and moved to Winstoke after a year at catering college. His parents had moved away years prior and the last Penny had heard, they'd both passed away shortly after Christmas.

"Within a few days of one another, apparently," she added sadly.

Derek and his wife, Janet, hadn't had any children. Now it seemed as though Janet had been left all alone. Although no one was truly alone in Hampsworthy Downs. It was a tight knit, friendly community and if she needed or wanted company or support, then there would be numerous people who would come to her aid.

As they approached the scene of the crime, Penny could see directly to the food tent through the diminishing crowd. Watching Monroe intently was Alan Dubois. He was standing next to Linda Green, who was wiping her hands on a damp cloth, and both were being questioned by a police constable. Alan had his arms folded, nose in the air, as aloof as ever, but Penny immediately noticed his immaculate attire was marred by a dark green grass stain on his right knee.

Tony Deacon was sitting on a hay bale, staring at his feet while being interviewed by John Monroe. There was a pile of arrows next to him. A constable was carefully gathering up the bows and placing them in evidence bags. He also collected the arrows and did likewise.

They're taking no chances, Penny thought.

Momentarily, Tony Deacon was accompanied by an officer to a waiting police car and John sauntered over to her. Susie tactfully walked away.

"Penny, I'm going to need you to come down to the station to make an official statement."

"Yes, of course. Do you want me to come now?"

Monroe shook his head.

"I'll be tied up with the immediate aftermath for a while yet. It's the most important part of the investigation, as no doubt you know? Within the next couple of days will be okay. If you give me a ring and let me know when to expect you, I'll take your statement myself." He laid a comforting hand on her shoulder. "Don't look so worried. You're a witness, not a suspect."

"Yes, I know that. I think I'm still in mild shock."

"I think so too. Go and get a cup of tea and sit down somewhere. Will you be all right?"

Penny looked up into his eyes and nodded.

"Yes, I'll be fine. Have you arrested Tony Deacon?" she asked, looking over to the police vehicle where the man was sitting in the back seat.

"No. We're just taking him to the station to give his statement. Between you and me, at the moment we don't know if this was a terrible accident or deliberate. But it warrants a full investigation either way. I'll see you soon, Penny. Go and get yourself a drink and be with your family."

"I will. Thanks, John."

Once the DI had left, Susie wandered back.

"You okay?"

Penny nodded, and they walked back to her parents. Sheila hugged her, rubbing her back like she used to when Penny was a child, and Albert put his arm around her shoulder. While Fischer's tail wagged hard against her leg. She bent down to give him a cuddle. Penny noticed her parents looked traumatised.

"Your mother thinks we should go home, Penny," her dad said. "We're going to call for a taxi now. I think we've all had enough excitement for one day. Do you want to come with us?"

"I'll stay with Susie for a bit. We can come back together later with the kids and Fischer."

"All right. But look after yourself, you've had a nasty shock, love."

After waving her parents off, Penny and Susie returned to the field. The fairground rides had started up again, and the music blared out above the shrieks and laughter. Penny wandered over to the archery range, deep in thought.

With all the bows and arrows removed, and Tony Deacon taken to the station, it was nothing more than an avenue of neatly arranged bales of hay. The targets had been left. Large painted circles fixed to tripod stands.

From the shooting line, she peered at the food tent. Linda Green was walking back inside, her back to Penny. Penny gazed back at the target.

"What is it, Penny?" Susie asked.

"While those bows were certainly capable of reaching that target, and I saw several children struggling to pull back the string, the bows themselves weren't all that powerful, Susie. Besides, you wouldn't use high standard bows for kids and amateurs."

"What's your point?"

"I don't think the bows could have reached the food tent from here, no matter how good the archer was."

"Mmm, I'm not so sure. They didn't look like toys to me. Without these hay walls keeping everyone safe, they'd be quite dangerous."

"They might be dangerous enough to hurt someone at close range, I agree. But only a crack shot could have hit Derek Cotton in the neck from this distance."

"Oh, Penny, please don't say it. Surely it was just a horrible accident?"

Penny nodded.

"Possibly. But by the same token, Susie, it could very well have been deliberate."

FOUR

Penny awoke on Sunday morning with the sun streaming through a narrow gap in the curtains. She pushed her thick unruly hair away from her face and reached for the book she'd dropped on the covers as she'd drifted off to sleep the night before.

She'd lain awake for hours as her mind ran over and over the events of the previous day. And been so distracted she'd read several pages of a gripping crime thriller before realising she'd absorbed none of it. Twice she'd had to skip back a few pages to start again. Eventually, she gave up. When sleep finally took her, it had been close to half-past three.

She was still feeling tired, thick headed and groggy as she made her way down the stairs of her cottage to put the kettle on for her morning tea.

She said good morning to Fischer, who was waiting patiently at the back door, and let him out into the garden.

He must have returned to his downstairs bed at some point during the night. No doubt fed up with being disturbed by her restless night.

As she leaned against the worktop, waiting for the kettle to boil, she found she couldn't stop yawning. Her jaw was beginning to ache with the effort. Hopefully, a strong black tea would revive her and give her some much needed energy.

It was the second day of the Queen's birthday fair and she wasn't going to miss it, no matter how bone-weary and sluggish she felt. There was still a lot to see, the most exciting event being the huge parade of floats, which was a traditional custom on day two of the celebration. Susie's children, Ellen and Billy, were taking part this year and Penny would never forgive herself if she missed seeing them in their costumes. According to Susie, they were the best she'd ever made.

"Ready to go then, Fish Face?" Penny asked her little dog once she'd cleared away their breakfast dishes.

Fischer yapped excitedly, wagging his tail and spinning in a couple of circles. Penny laughed.

"I'll take that as a yes, then."

The village was quiet. The only person Penny saw on her way to the bus stop was the paperboy, his bag bulging with huge Sunday newspapers stuffed full of supplements and weekend magazines. Not to mention a thousand loose advertising leaflets, most of which would end up in the recycling bins.

Penny met up with Susie at the stop. Her friend had been waiting since she'd dropped Billy and Ellen off so they could get ready with their friends. She spent the wait for the bus chatting excitedly about the costumes and her kids' chances of winning.

The Ups and Downs bus arrived on time, and even though what had happened the previous day had been a shock for everyone, there was still a good crowd waiting to attend the second day of celebrations.

On the journey to Hampsworthy Downs, unlike the previous day when she'd been lively and full of energy, Penny felt herself nodding off. Head leaning against the window while Susie chatted on about something or other. The hedgerows flashing by were hypnotic, and it wasn't until they reached the sports field that she jolted awake.

"Welcome back to the land of the living," Susie said, grinning. "You've missed all the crowds lining up along the road to see the floats. They all got a good view of your squashed up face drooling against the window."

Penny burst out laughing.

"I did not!"

"Did too. Right, no more thinking about what happened yesterday. Let's get out there and have some fun, Penny Finch. Come on Fischer."

———•———

Stepping out into the warm morning air, Penny noticed immediately the cordon blocking off one side of the field was still in place. A pair of uniformed constables stood on guard, ensuring no one strayed onto what was obviously still being designated as a crime scene.

The tannoy once again crackled into life and Ted announced the parade of floats had just set off for its journey around Hambleton Chase village. It wouldn't be long before they began to arrive.

Penny and Susie grabbed a takeout cup of coffee each from a nearby vendor before making their way to line up at the entrance where the floats would come in. There was a massive crowd, all waving flags. Some dressed in the fancy dress of kings and queens of history, and many dressed as Queen Elizabeth II. One woman even held a real corgi in her arms. He was a placid little thing, quite happily taking everything in. Penny handed her coffee cup to Susie and lifted Fischer in her arms.

"Do you want to see what's happening as well, little man?"

He gave her nose a quick lick, then turned to watch the crowd with interest.

Suddenly the sound of a cheer from the end of the line rippled along until it reached them, and laughing, they joined in. The lead float had been spotted coming up the hill and would be turning into the gate any minute.

Highly decorated flat bed lorries from local businesses carried the fancy dress contestants. They were joined by local farmers driving their tractors and pulling trailers filled with competitors. There were many on foot pulling home-made hand carts, dressed as a vast array of figures. Some had charity buckets for spectators to throw their change in.

The local fire brigade engine drove to the entrance, its red and chrome bodywork gleaming in the sun and its blue light flashing slowly. The firemen and women proudly walking alongside.

Evans Dairy milk float came next, with the delivery boys sitting in the back on empty milk churns, wearing straw hats and overalls and chewing on lengths of straw.

But the main attractions were the children from the local schools in their year groups. A cheer went up from the crowd as they rumbled onto the field.

The infant school came first on a lorry that had been decorated as a summer garden. The children were dressed as flowers, bees, fairies, rabbits, and garden gnomes.

"Oh look how sweet they all are," Penny said to Susie.

Each high school year had taken a different theme. The eldest group had chosen environmental awareness, and carried brightly painted banners urging action to save Hampsworthy Downs from pollution.

Another year had taken the theme of a Victorian school, and one of the pupils was dressed as a severe looking head mistress, with half-moon glasses, a wig of Grey hair done up in a tight bun, a long cane and an exaggerated scowl on her face. Her pupils showed various messages marked on old fashioned school slates.

"Look, Penny," Susie said, nudging her in the ribs. "Ellen and Billy are coming."

The last float was decorated like a castle. Grey crenellations around the edge of the lorry had been painted to look like old stone walls. A tower at the front, behind the driver's cab, contained two children dressed as the Queen and Prince Philip. They were standing proudly and giving expert royal waves to the sea of onlookers.

On the back of the lorry Ellen was dressed as Elizabeth I and next to her was Billy, who had come as Charles I, with his head under his arm. Underneath the ruff at the neck of the costume, which was actually sat on his head, Penny could see Billy grinning as he waved excitedly.

"Susie, they look brilliant! I love that head."

"No one wanted to be King Charles," Susie said. "But Billy jumped at the chance. He's been reading all about the civil war and the political and military conflicts. He loves all the gore, unfortunately. It was his idea to go without a head. I only hope he doesn't throw it on the crowd, which is where the real Charles's head ended up."

"Boys love all the blood and guts of history. I see it at the library all the time."

"You know, we've been making that head all week. Billy really enjoyed it."

"You've both done a fantastic job, Susie."

Penny could clearly see the head of the king painted on the front. Realistically sculpted ears and a nose, and a tongue lolling out of the side of the mouth. It really was very well done.

Susie grimaced.

"He insisted on adding the tongue. I honestly thought the teachers would say no, but they were quite happy for him to go ahead."

"It shows his creative side," Penny said. "Personally, I think he should get extra marks for that. In fact, and I know I'm biased, but I think he should win. His costume is, forgive the pun, head and shoulders above the rest."

Susie laughed.

"Billy said exactly the same thing. About winning, I mean, not your joke. Very good joke, though."

After the final float had passed, the vast crowd that had lined the route followed them in, and Penny and Susie joined the swelling number to walk into the main area. There would now be a nail biting wait for the contestants, teachers and parents while the judges made their rounds.

Eventually, Old Ted on the tannoy announced the judges were about to make their final decisions. Penny felt Susie tense up beside her as the judges, a group of local dignitaries, approached the float her children were on.

"I hope Billy at least gets a ribbon," Susie said. "If only for that grotesque head. It took days to make. I shredded a load of James' old newspapers for the paper mache. He kept them stacked up in the garage, tied in bundles. Shelf after shelf of the stupid things, refusing to throw them out no matter how many times I asked him. He said they were a documentation of our country's history and would be worth something one day. For a clever man, he had a weird idea of a good investment. He said he'd be back to collect them, but

I've had enough of storing them all. I've lost count of how many times I've either had to move them or tripped over them while trying to get something done in the garage. I bet the only reason he's not come and got them is because his new girlfriend won't have them in the house. I should have got rid of them years ago. Actually, I should have got rid of him years ago, too."

Penny looked at her friend and saw the sadness in her eyes. James had left Susie and the children a while ago now, but the pain of the separation for Susie sometimes seemed as fresh and raw as the day it had happened. But, Penny thought to herself, the fact Susie had disposed of James' newspaper collection was a sign she was finally moving on.

"We wouldn't have Billy or Ellen if you'd got rid of James, Susie."

Susie nodded and smiled gratefully.

"Yes, you're right. They make all the bad times worthwhile."

They looked back at the float and watched as Ellen gave them an enthusiastic wave, followed by a classic royal one which made them laugh.

"Penny, look!"

Billy was being awarded a gold ribbon by the judges, and with a huge grin, he held the head aloft like a sports trophy, waving it in triumph.

"First place, Susie, that's fantastic. He's getting his prizes now, too. Do you know what they are this year?"

"Book tokens, which he'll love, and a new tablet. I think there are some games as well, donated from the toy shop in

Winstoke. I'm so pleased for him, Penny. It makes using up all my flour more than worth it. No cake for after dinner today, but I don't think they will mind."

"Actually, I had a bit of a baking session recently and have a few cupcakes left. I'll bring them over for you later."

"Brilliant, thanks, Penny."

With the judging over, Billy and Ellen raced across the field to their mother, talking ten to the dozen about their trip around the village on the back of the lorry, Billy's win and the fantastic prizes he'd been given. Penny and Susie grinned and nodded in what they hoped were appropriate places, unable to get a word in edgeways. Fischer barked in excitement and was awarded with hugs and kisses from them all, as well as a few of his favourite treats.

Penny and Susie spent the rest of the day wandering around the fairground. Taking turns to accompany Billy and Ellen on the rides while the other looked after Fischer. They purchased knick-knacks and gifts from the pop-up shops. Penny, succumbing to the tea pots she'd fallen for the previous day, bought both the cauliflower and the hot-air balloon shaped ones, much to the delight of the stallholder who remembered her from the day before.

They had lunch at a tented cafe and took afternoon tea at bistro tables set outside a converted horse box. Scattered straw on the ramp gave it a genuine look, but the box smelled of delicious cakes, coffee and tea as opposed to something a lot more unpalatable. The two friends relaxed and chatted while watching the children at the face-painting booth next door. Billy returned looking like a fierce dragon, while Ellen had opted for the Queen of Hearts from Alice in Wonderland.

"Shall we take one more circuit of the field, then call it a day?" Susie asked, stifling a yawn.

Penny agreed. It was only early afternoon, but it was amazing how tired a body could get when doing nothing of importance. Especially after a poor night's sleep.

As they wandered, Penny found herself glancing several times at the area where Fischer had alerted everyone to the body. It was still cordoned off with a single uniformed constable guarding the perimeter, but all signs of this being the spot where a serious crime had taken place had been removed. She frowned, puzzling over what could have happened, but was unable to make sense of it. Eventually Susie nudged her.

"Stop thinking about it, Penny. I know that brain of yours won't rest until you know what transpired, but can't we just enjoy the last hour of the fair without thinking about crime scenes and murder?"

"Sorry. Yes, you're right. Come on. How about one last go on the bumper cars? I've just seen Mr Kelly. I'm sure he'll be more than happy to look after Fischer for ten minutes while we take the kids."

"You're on. Prepare to be beaten."

"I don't doubt it for a second, Susie. I've seen the way you drive."

FIVE

All five of them fell asleep on the Ups and Downs return journey. Fischer was curled up on Penny's knee and she had Ellen leaning against her shoulder. Across the aisle, Billy had his head resting on his mum's knee while Susie herself was gently snoring, head resting against the window. By the time they alighted in Cherrytree Downs, the only one who wasn't covered in smudged face paint was Fischer.

Penny and Susie took one look at the kid's faces and burst out laughing. They now resembled a pair of angry storm clouds.

"Come on, you two," Susie said. "Let's go home and get you both cleaned up."

"I'll come over in a couple of hours," Penny said.

"You're welcome to come for dinner, you know."

"Thanks, but I've already got a casserole prepared and I need to give Fischer his dinner. I'll come for desert, though."

"As long as you remember to bring it with you, otherwise you'll be sorely disappointed."

Penny laughed.

"I wouldn't dare forget it."

The short walk from the bus stop back to Penny's cottage took twice as long as normal, while she waited for Fischer to sniff every blade of grass and tree on the way.

Two hours later, both fed and rested, she and Fischer ventured out again, the promised cupcakes in a box, to walk over to Susie's house. It was still bright and warm, with the excitement of the weekend's festivities still palpable. She could hear laughter and music from several houses, as neighbours, friends and families gathered together for BBQs in the garden.

Billy and Ellen flung open the door as she and Fischer walked down the path. Full of excited non-stop chatter, which was their default mode, their faces scrubbed clean and beaming. Penny noticed Billy still had his gold ribbon in his hand and said as much to Susie.

"As long as he puts it down long enough to get ready for bed."

The children erupted in protest at the sound of the word 'bed.'

"Don't panic, it's not bedtime yet. Why don't you take Fischer into the lounge while I make Penny a cup of tea?"

"Here, I've brought you a cupcake each," Penny said, opening the box.

"Yum! Thank you, Penny," both kids chorused, taking one each and returning to their games, Penny's little dog trotting after them happily.

"Don't give Fischer any, please," Penny added. "It's not good for him."

"We won't."

In the kitchen, drinking tea and munching on cupcakes, Susie turned to Penny and told her she'd been doing some digging into the murder. Starting with those people she knew were in the vicinity at the time. Susie was a reporter with the Winstoke Gazette, so had a few avenues she could explore that Penny could not.

"Oh? What did you find out?"

"Were you aware that Alan Dubois had a fairly illustrious sporting past?"

Penny shook her head. She didn't know Dubois particularly well. She'd read several of his restaurant reviews and had heard him a few times being interviewed on local radio stations while driving in her library van, but that was the sum-total of her knowledge. He didn't strike her as a sportsman.

"What sport did he play?"

"I'm not sure play is the right word," Susie said, pausing for effect. "He was a world class archer."

Penny returned her cup to its saucer carefully and stared at her friend. She felt a cold shiver run up her spine.

"Archery? That is a surprise. How did you find out?"

"I did an internal archive search at work, that's all. I was expecting mainly to read reports about his work as a restaurant critic, but found some additional links to an old interview he did and there it was. Dubois was an archer and competed in the 2002 Manchester commonwealth games."

"He must have been really good?"

"He was. He won a bronze medal that year and could have gone on to represent team GB at the Olympics, but had to pull out at the last minute and lost his spot. You'll never believe the reason why."

Penny shook her head. She couldn't even fathom a guess.

"Food poisoning."

"No! Really?"

"Yep. It was a bad meal in one of those national pub chains. That's when he started his work as a food critic. I can see the reason why he did, but can't understand why he never competed again. Like you say, he was obviously good at it." Susie lifted the teapot. "Do you want a top up?"

Penny shook her head and pushed back her chair.

"No thanks, Susie. I'm going to call John Monroe. He needs to know what you've learned. Unless you want to tell him?" Penny added, hoping her friend would say no.

Susie smirked.

"I'll leave it to you. I wouldn't want to deprive you of an excuse to talk to your favourite detective."

"It's not like that, Susie."

"I'm your best friend and have known you all my life, Penny Finch. That's exactly how it is. A blind man on a galloping horse in a snowstorm can see how attracted you are to one another. I don't know why you don't both just admit it and get on with it. Let's be realistic, Penny. Neither of you are in the first bloom of youth. No offense. Stop wasting time and start enjoying life together while you can."

Penny sighed.

"All right, I admit there is something there. But I want to take it slowly, Susie. I don't want to rush into anything and find out I've made a dreadful mistake. Look what happened with Edward."

Susie got up and gave her friend a hug.

"Sorry. You're right. You need to go at your own pace. But, believe me, John Monroe is absolutely nothing like your ex. I'll wager you'll both be a couple by the end of the year. You're made for one another. And if you listen to me, it could be by the end of the month."

"I'm not taking that bet, Susie. But, thank you. I'll see you later."

The children, hearing Penny was leaving, rushed into the hall to say goodbye, Fischer hot on their heels. Penny clipped on his lead and with hugs all round, left to walk home.

The village was quieter now, with everyone worn out after a long weekend of celebration and community events. She let Fischer off his lead at the village green, where he ran about sniffing and visited his favourite tree. While he was busy exploring, Penny pulled out her phone and called John. After a couple of rings, it was answered.

"John Monroe," a deep timbered voice answered in a professional tone.

"John, it's Penny."

"Penny," he said, his voice brightening audibly. "Sorry, I didn't look at the screen. I didn't realise it was you. How can I help?"

"I've just found out some information from Susie and thought you should know. Alan Dubois was a competitive archer."

She told him what Susie had discovered, then fell silent, waiting for a response.

Monroe didn't speak for a moment, but Penny could hear the faint sounds of a pen scratching on paper while he took notes.

"Listen," he replied eventually. "I know it's getting late, but could I come over and take your statement while it's all still fresh in your memory? This new information is important, and I'd like to get everything down as soon as possible."

"Of course."

"Thanks, Penny. I'll see you in about an hour."

———•———

Penny stood in her front room, looking out of the window. Fischer was sitting on the window ledge, also gazing outside, but with no idea, as yet, what they were looking for. Even though dusk was falling and the light was disappearing as she watched, Penny's garden still looked cheerful and inviting, filled as it was with colourful blooms. The bunting, which she'd strung from the upstairs windows down to the hedge on either side of the path, swung in a gentle breeze. But as much as she loved her garden, Penny didn't really notice it this evening. She was waiting for Monroe to arrive.

As the last vestiges of light sunk below the horizon, Penny switched on the tiffany lamps either side of the sofa. Then Fischer's tail began to wag furiously and he let out a delighted yelp just as she saw the flash of a car's headlights at the end of her road.

Fischer's tail wagged even faster, and he began to bark. Penny looked at him and gave him an ear scratch. Her clever little dog had known before even she was sure. Monroe was here.

Penny willed herself to walk slowly to the door, despite the involuntary excited churning in her stomach. She briefly stopped at the hall mirror to check her unruly hair. She attempted to smooth it down with her hands, but despite her endeavors, it sprang back into its normal semi bird's nest. She sighed, wondering why she was bothering. A quick glance at Fischer's quizzical face told her he was thinking the same thing.

"I know, little man. What on earth am I doing?"

She opened the door to John's recognisable rat-a-tat-tat and smiled.

"Hello, John. Please, come in."

"Hi, Penny. Thanks for seeing me so late."

"No problem. Do you want a cup of tea?"

"I'd rather get your statement out of the way first, if you don't mind?" he replied, bending to make a fuss of the little dog who was frantically climbing up his trouser leg in a bid to be noticed.

"Of course. Come through to the kitchen. We can sit at the table."

Monroe sat, opened his briefcase, and retrieved an official statement form. Twisting the cap off his pen, he began filling in the date, time and interviewee details. Penny noticed how his hand moved swiftly but precisely across the page, leaving a perfectly legible trail of ink in a well practiced cursive.

"If this is an official form, shouldn't you use my proper name?" she asked.

Monroe looked at her quizzically. She indicated the page.

"My full name is Penelope."

He rolled his eyes and gave her a wry look and a lopsided grin. Picking up the form, he neatly tore it in half.

"It's been a long weekend. I'm not thinking straight. When I think of you, it's always as Penny. Let me get another form."

He bent down and, putting the ripped paper halves back in his case, retrieved another, unaware of the effect his words had had on Penny.

'When I think of you.'

Her heart gave a thump, and she felt herself blush slightly.

"Right, let me start again," John said, filling out the form with her name in full. "Now, tell me how you discovered the victim."

"I was chasing Fischer."

Fischer looked up from his bed at his name being mentioned.

"He was running away? That doesn't sound like Fischer. What happened?"

Penny shook her head.

"I'm not sure exactly. He wasn't running away though, he was running towards Derek Cotton. I remember the civil reenactment society had sounded a volley early and Ted had just finished apologising on their behalf when Fischer bolted. He'd been in the middle of competing in the dog show when something caused him to run. I thought it was the musket firing at first that had frightened him, but I think he'd seen Derek fall and that was where he was headed."

"All right. What happened next?"

"I didn't realise what had happened, or who it was until I was there. I saw the arrow sticking out of his neck and the blood spreading across his shirt. I may have called out for someone to ring an ambulance. No, actually, I think that was dad. I can't remember if I said anything at all now I think about it. I picked Fischer up though. I do remember that. I was afraid he was going to bolt into the road."

"Was Derek moving at all?"

"No. He was just lying there, completely still. I knew he was dead, John. It was obvious. If I thought for one moment there was even a slight chance he was still alive, I would have tried to do something."

John nodded.

"I know you would. I'm sorry, but I have to ask these questions. I'm not doubting your integrity. I know how much of a shock you must have had. If you want to do this another time, I fully understand."

"No. I'm okay. I need to tell you all I know while I can remember it."

John smiled.

"Thanks, Penny. So, had you seen Derek Cotton prior to finding him dead?"

"Yes. I was in the food marquee about half an hour before, and Derek was there giving out samples of food to promote his bistro in Winstoke."

"Who else was there?"

"Amanda. She's the receptionist at The Rough Spot. The veterinarian practice I take Fischer to. She was selling her homemade cakes. Alan Dubois, the food critic, and Linda Green were also there. Janet Cotton, Derek's wife, was leaving just as I entered."

"I've had reports that Derek and his wife were arguing. Did you see anything like that?"

Penny shook her head.

"Not much, really. Janet said something along the lines of not staying in the tent with him, and I heard Derek shout out, 'until death do us part, my dear.' Or something like that. It's a bit fuzzy, to be honest."

"Okay. Let us move on to Alan Dubois. You found out from Susie tonight that he is an experienced archer?"

"That's right. He won a bronze medal at the 2002 commonwealth games, apparently."

"Did you see him with a bow at any point during the fair? Prior to the time Derek was found, I mean?"

Penny paused, thinking back.

"No, but I did see him sneak round the back of the marquee, which struck me as odd. He looked a bit furtive. Did you know he had experience with a bow?"

Monroe leaned back in his chair and shook his head.

"No, I didn't. We'd have found out soon enough, but I'm grateful for the information so quickly. I'll be asking him about it when I interview him. As a witness," he added, with emphasis. He handed Penny his pen and slid across the statement. "Would you have a read through what I've written and sign it if you're happy that it's all correct and as you remember?"

Penny read it through, impressed at how accurately and succinctly John Monroe had put her words together. She reached the end and signed, finding her hand was shaking slightly.

Monroe took back the pen as she offered it, then held her hand.

"You're shaking. Don't worry, Penny, we'll find out what happened."

"I know you will," she replied, not disclosing the real reason she was trembling. "Can I get you that tea now?" she asked as he put away the pen and her completed statement. Snapping his briefcase shut with a satisfying click.

"If I'm not in your way, then that would be very welcome. I'm not officially on duty, although as a DI on a serious case, I suppose I'm never really off duty."

"Has Tony Deacon been of any help?" Penny asked as she filled the kettle and switched it on.

"Not really. He said he was gathering up the used arrows down by the target on the range when he heard the musket go off. Even if he had been at the end of the range, it's unlikely he could have shot Cotton."

"Oh? Why's that?" Penny asked.

"We've been testing the bows and they're only capable of travelling a certain distance. Enough to hit the target from the start line at the fair's booth, fifteen or twenty metres, to give people a fair chance, but no further. From what I saw of the wound, and the post-mortem has corroborated my thoughts although it hasn't been made official yet, the force of impact means someone would have had to have been within ten feet of the victim to deliver the fatal shot."

"Not the fifteen or twenty metres from the range."

John nodded.

"Precisely. We've been pouring over the details all weekend and the results of the experiments are always the same. I'll be making a formal statement tomorrow, but just so you know, it's now officially a murder inquiry."

SIX

The night had passed in what felt like the briefest of moments, and now Penny's room was bathed in bright morning sunshine. She was still as tired as she had been when she'd gone to bed, but she threw back the covers and shook off the fatigue before venturing downstairs for breakfast.

With Fischer outside in the back garden taking care of his morning business, she shook a natural, organic muesli into a bowl and, covering it with almond milk, stood with her back to the kitchen counter to eat while she waited for the kettle to boil.

Fischer scurried in a few moments later and ate his own breakfast, while Penny finished hers and sipped her coffee. She needed all the energy she could find this morning. Luckily, she'd had time to make today's lunch and put it in the fridge before John Monroe had arrived the night before.

Quarter of an hour later she and Fischer were outside ready to begin the day.

"Come on, up you get, Fish Face," she said. "We don't want to be late."

Penny prided herself on always being in the correct place and on time with her mobile library. Her customers had come to expect it and she didn't want to let them down. For many of the elderly residents in the six villages and hamlets that made up Hampsworthy Downs, a visit to the mobile library was their main social activity and a weekly chance to meet up with friends. She wasn't prepared to disappoint any of them.

Monday morning's first stop was Rowan Downs, only a short drive from her own village of Cherrytree Downs, and as usual her first visitors of the week were the indefatigable ladies of the village, Mrs Lillian Greaves and Mrs Harriet Ward. They were quarrelling about something as usual. If there was ever a day when they weren't exchanging a few 'words,' Penny knew one of them would be ill and probably in need of a doctor.

Penny was expecting them and already had their book choice for this week on the counter. Heaven forbid they should ever request a book she only had one copy of. They always wanted the same book, every week, no matter how obscure the title. As they stepped up into the van, Penny produced two copies of Elizabeth & Margaret: The Intimate World of the Windsor Sisters. It was a biography of the Queen and her sister written by royal biographer Andrew Morton. It was one of Penny's own favourites. Wonderfully written and meticulously researched, it gave a fascinating insight into the world of the royal sisters and the dynamic between them.

Lillian and Harriet were silent for a moment as they both took hold of their books with an almost worshipful reverence.

"Thank you, Penny," Harriet said.

"Yes, thank you very much, my dear," Lillian said, eager not to be outdone by her friend.

"I'm glad I could help," Penny said. "It was a bit tricky getting two copies, especially on the Queen's birthday weekend. It has proved to be a very popular title this week."

"We had every confidence in you," Lillian said. "Didn't we, Harriet?"

"Oh, we did. You've never let us down once in all the years we've been visiting your library."

And Penny dreaded the day she ever did let them down. But today they were happy and as they left and wended their way back home, Penny could hear the two of them chatting. Although mild bickering was probably a better description.

Her next customer was a relative new-comer to the village, Ms Scarlett, the new owner of the local fish and chip shop, Chips Ahoy. As a former actress, she was more than aptly named. She walked with natural grace and style Penny admitted to herself she was a little envious of. She looked down at her own jeans and tee shirt with a sigh. No matter what she wore, even if it was expensive silk and diamonds, she'd never achieve the elegance of Chase Scarlett. Who would look fantastic if she was dressed in nothing more than a bin bag.

She reached under the counter and withdrew a slim volume. It was a play Ms Scarlett had asked her for and she'd found it in the main library.

"Oh, you found it, Penny. Very well done."

"I did," Penny replied, holding up a copy of The Birthday Party by Harold Pinter.

"I once played the part of Lulu, you know," Chase said, waving her arm dramatically. "But I realise now, in my more seasoned years, I would probably be better suited to the part of Meg."

"I'm sure you'd impress in any part, Chase," Penny said. And she meant it. Chase Scarlett was born for the stage. It was only a domino effect of adverse circumstances that had brought her to where she was now.

"I'm not performing this time, my darling. I'm reading it ahead of the local amateur dramatics society production. They've asked me to direct," she said with a note of pride.

"How wonderful," Penny replied. "You will save a ticket for me, won't you?"

"Indubitably, darling. Ciao for now," she said and swept away with a rustle of chiffon, leaving behind a cloud of sweet, floral scent.

After a pleasant morning at Rowan Downs, the library moved onto Chiddingborne for the afternoon session. The day was warm, and the countryside was filled with the gentle sounds of summer. Somewhere across the downs a farmer was driving his tractor as they did every day at this time of the year, and the regular thrum of the engine drifted over the hedgerows as Penny made her way along the quiet country road to her next stop.

Before opening the library for the afternoon, Penny took Fischer for a walk then ate her lunch on a bench close to the village green. A pair of young boys were working on the church notice board, rubbing down the wood and applying a fresh coat of varnish, before finally re-pinning the notices and closing the glass front. Penny watched them work as she ate. Fischer, stretched out on his back beneath the bench, gave a big yawn, as though the sight of the two youths working hard in the heat of the day had thoroughly worn him out.

Back at the library, Penny opened the doors to let out the heat which had accumulated, then set up her folding chair and table outside while she waited for her first customers. Even though she was warmed by the sun, Penny felt an inexplicable chill come over her when she spied Linda Green stomping towards the library. She expected her to walk past, but to her surprise, Linda stopped. She wasn't a regular at the mobile library and Penny didn't really know her. They'd not exchanged more than half a dozen words in as many years.

"I have a card for the <u>proper</u> library," Linda said. "Can I use it here?"

Penny felt herself bristle slightly at Linda's emphasis on the word proper, but perhaps it was a simple misunderstanding.

"Of course," she said cheerfully. "Just think of the campervan as a mobile extension of the main branch in Winstoke."

"Like my home made jam samples are an extension of my own kitchen?"

"Exactly. So, what can I help you with? Are you looking for something in particular?"

"It's probably a bit of a tall order, but I was hoping to find something on Japanese cuisine. I want to develop my skills and expand my range a bit."

Penny knew she had one old recipe book in the cookery section that had a chapter on classic Japanese dishes. She stepped up into the van to search for it.

"I do have one that might be of interest. It's actually a vegetarian cook book, but as there are a lot of vegetarian dishes in Japan, there's a full chapter dedicated to it."

Linda laughed.

"All right, I'll take a look. Although, I personally think no meal is complete without a healthy portion of meat."

As a vegetarian herself, Penny could have argued the point, but that wasn't her job. She handed the book to Linda with a smile.

"But I am open to trying new things," she added, thumbing through the pages. "My school teachers said I was bad at tests and I failed my exams, but I've never ever had one of my meals returned to the kitchen. Just goes to show exams aren't everything, doesn't it?"

"You worked at Bistro 23, didn't you? I saw you at the fair in the food marquee."

"Yes, I saw you too. Right before Derek Cotton died. I've had the police asking me questions all weekend."

"Did you happen to see anything?" Penny asked.

"I left my stall. I was," she hesitated for a second. "Away when I heard the musket go off. When I got back, there were police everywhere and Derek Cotton was dead."

"I heard you say to Derek that he'd stolen your recipes?"

"He did. He knew absolutely nothing about food, and even less about running a business. He let me run the kitchen. He couldn't even make cheese on toast without burning it. I'd been there a few months when I noticed he was hanging around the kitchen a lot more, asking me questions and being all kind and friendly. It was only after he'd had to let me go that I realised he'd been only been nice because he wanted all my recipes. I'd devised a lot of those myself and they were excellent. I liked working at the bistro. I could set the menus and experiment to develop my own dishes. All I had to do in return was put up with a horrible boss."

"Why did he ask you to leave?"

"He said it was financial reasons. Which was rubbish. I know the bistro wasn't doing that well, but I think he just wanted to get someone cheaper in. I hadn't even been gone a day before he took on a kid straight out of catering college and took on the head chef position himself. And he was using all my recipes. The cheek! I could have killed him."

Linda flushed and bit her lip the moment she'd realised what she'd said.

"I know," Penny said. "Just a figure of speech?"

Linda tucked the recipe book under her arm and handed Penny her library card.

"Are you still out of work since you left the bistro?" Penny asked, taking the card details and handing it back to Linda.

"I get by with my home-made jams and breads. A few stalls at farmer's markets and the main weekly market in Winstoke. But I hope to have my own kitchen very soon."

"Oh? Anywhere nice?"

"The duel carriageway around Winstoke. I'm getting a burger van."

"A burger van?" Penny asked, unable to keep the surprise from her voice.

Linda bristled, obviously taking offense.

"It might not be my dream kitchen, but truckers love a burger and it can be good money. I'll save enough for my own restaurant one day."

"Of course. But you must miss working in a proper kitchen."

"Do you miss working in a proper library?" Linda replied, sticking out her chin in defiance. Challenging Penny to respond.

Penny was instantly chastened. Her library van was more than just a job. She loved the freedom it gave her, being able to travel around providing a much-needed service to the residents, while being her own boss. There was no difference between what she was doing and what Linda wanted to do.

"Linda, I am so sorry. I didn't mean that the way it came out. I'm sure you'll do a great job wherever you work."

"I will. I'm looking forward to setting up on my own. Maybe Cotton did me a favour by letting me go. At least one other good thing besides dropping dead."

Penny detected Linda's hint of a smile, cold and spiteful, before the woman turned and left.

As she watched her walk away, Penny was struck by one thing. Linda Green was not at all sorry Derek Cotton was dead.

SEVEN

Penny drove the mobile library out to Hambleton Chase the next morning. It was the closest village to the scene of the crime and although she'd tried hard to cast it from her mind, she just couldn't forget about the murder.

She drove on with Fischer sitting in the passenger seat, happily gazing at the scenery and sniffing at the tantalising country smells wafting in through the open window.

Tuesdays always felt like the longest day of the week for Penny. The library was in the village for the whole day, so there wasn't a break to relocate to a second stop. In many ways, it was the easiest day of the week, and when the weather was as glorious as it was today, she could sit out on her camping chair and read or play with her little dog while she waited for her customers.

As with all the other villages, Tuesday's patrons were made up mostly of her regulars, the library being a main feature of their week. They always came to return the previous week's books and select their next ones. Stopping for a chat with Penny, to play with Fischer and ask him to do his repertoire of tricks for treats, which they always kept in their pockets just for him, and to stop and chat with their friends. The mobile library was the social hub for many village residents. It was so much part of their routine that Penny could almost set her watch by the arrival of certain customers.

Mrs Reed always turned up shortly after Penny had opened. The old lady could see the van arrive from her kitchen window, and Penny would often see her waiting there. She'd give her a wave, then park the van, and a few minutes later Mrs Reed would amble over just as Penny was opening the doors.

Mr Gough always came just before lunch. Every time Penny would think it was time to close up so she could take Fischer for a walk and eat her sandwich, Mr Gough would appear. Red-cheeked and perspiring, always out of breath for the first few minutes while he selected a historical action adventure novel.

"Made it just in time, again," Mr Gough said today. He was mopping his brow with a red and white spotted handkerchief as he handed Penny his library card.

Penny couldn't understand why he didn't arrive a bit earlier, or even wait until after lunch. But Mr Gough had been arriving in the same manner, rushing to be the last customer before her first break, for so long now that it was probably an indelible part of his schedule.

"You know, there's no need to rush, Mr. Gough," Penny said, fearing for his heart as well as his blood pressure. "I'm happy to wait for you."

"Oh, I left home in plenty of time today. I just got distracted with watching the police come and go from the sports field," he replied, tucking his handkerchief in his trouser pocket.

"Are they still examining the area?"

"Not anymore. All the police tape has been removed and they've just started to take down the last of the tents left over from the fair. It will be all back to normal soon. I wonder if they've found any clues?" He glanced around, then leaned in closer to Penny. "I did hear the victim was killed by a former employee at Bistro 23. She was angry when he sacked her, by all accounts."

Penny sighed inwardly at how quickly and efficiently the gossip mongers had got to work. Could there be a kernel of truth in the rumours? The only former employee she knew of was Linda Green. She was obviously bitter and angry at Derek Cotton, and Penny had witnessed the altercation between the two of them. But was she really experienced enough with a bow to shoot a lethal arrow, which by all accounts could only have been achieved by a crack shot?

After Mr Gough had said goodbye and wandered off, far more slowly than the manner in which he'd arrived, Penny shut up the library. She stood thinking for a minute, then looked down at the little dog sitting by her feet, wondering what was going on. Why weren't they going for a walk?

"Come on, Fish Face. Back in the van. We're having a change today. I think a walk around the sports field is called for, and it's too far to walk there and back in our lunch hour."

Although Penny had spent many hours wandering around the field over the celebration weekend, today it was totally unrecognisable as the bustling party atmosphere it had been. The field was huge and only one corner was still occupied. The archery range and the food marquee had been closed off by the police, but now all the equipment was being dismantled and removed. A big flat bed lorry was being loaded with the hay bales that had been used as safety walls for the range, and the large marquee was being emptied as another crew stood by in readiness to drop the heavy canvas walls and dismantle the frame.

After walking a section of the perimeter to give Fischer his exercise, Penny sat on the grass to watch the activity and eat her lunch. She had sandwiches made from the last of the cheesy, crusted loaf she had baked herself, filled with sweet cherry tomatoes from her dad's greenhouse.

Fischer, sitting patiently beside her, cocked his head to one side and gave a little whine. Cheese was his favourite. She took one of his treats from her bag and he lay down to chew happily.

With their lunch finished, Penny packed up and she and Fischer started to wander back to the van. Passing the hay bales, she could see they were not simply stacked on top of one another as he'd initially assumed, but pinned in place by large steel bars. Moving on, she suddenly realised she was standing in almost the exact spot where Derek Cotton had died and gave an involuntary shudder.

Half way back to the library van, Penny saw Janet Cotton walking across the field with a large box in her arms, en route from the food tent to her car, which was parked on the field a short distance away. Janet averted her eyes when she saw the librarian. Penny frowned and changed direction, approaching Janet as she was loading the box into the boot of her vehicle. Janet slammed the lid shut and looked at Penny with a scowl.

"Janet, I just want to say how sorry I am about what happened to Derek."

"Don't be. I'm not. Good riddance to him, as far as I'm concerned."

Penny was a little taken aback at Janet's vehement tone. It was obvious she and her husband had fallen out of love, but they'd spent many years together. He'd been a big part of her life. Surely she would feel something, other than glad, that he had died? Especially in such an awful way. Penny knew she would if her husband had died suddenly, no matter how estranged they'd become. Even though she and Edward were no longer a couple, she would still feel sorry if his life was cut short.

"What will you do now? Will you keep Bistro 23 open?"

"Not that it's any of your business, Penny, but I'm selling the restaurant," she yanked open the driver's side door of her car. "And I'm selling off all this kitchen junk," she added, indicating the boxes stacked in the boot. "That way, I should be able to pay off all the debts that my idiot husband racked up." She got in the car and reached for the door handle to pull it closed, but hesitated a moment, looking at Penny. "The police tell me it's now a murder inquiry. Well, as far as I'm concerned, it couldn't have happened to a more deserving person."

Penny gasped. This was taking bitterness to a whole new level. Janet Cotton had obviously hated her husband.

"Have you any idea who may have wanted him dead?" she asked.

Janet looked at her and smirked.

"Did you even meet Derek? I can't imagine anyone meeting him who didn't want him dead. I'm just glad he died before he went bankrupt and left us completely penniless. If I'm lucky, I can get out of all this debt and still keep my house."

"But I always assumed the bistro was popular and doing well. How could he have been in such serious financial difficulty?"

Janet closed the car door and started the engine. Penny thought she'd gone too far with her questions and the woman would simply drive away, but Janet wound down the window.

"I don't know why I'm telling you all this," she said.

Penny didn't know either, but she didn't want her to stop. The more information she found out, the more she could pass on to John.

"That business was the only thing he cared about," Janet said savagely. "Every single penny we ever made was poured back into that stupid kitchen. He called it an investment. I called it an obsession. And you know something else? He couldn't even cook! But I suppose anyone can make money with a hobby these days. He was always on about when he opened his second restaurant. That he'd move to London and be the big shot. The way he talked you'd think he was going to be the next host of master chef. The man was a complete and utter deluded fool."

"Did the business suffer because Alan Dubois gave it a bad review?" Penny asked quickly, seeing that Janet's leaving was imminent.

She eyed Penny while pulling on her seat belt.

"Derek would never let me look at the accounts. Even though I know my way around a spreadsheet far better than him and could have done the accounts with my eyes shut, he was both arrogant and secretive about it. But, I don't think the review made the slightest difference. The bistro had its regulars, and they kept coming back. What really got Derek's goat was the perceived insult. Alan Dubois is well known for writing scathing reviews, yet Derek, with his smug and cocky attitude, was convinced he'd give him a good review. Of course he didn't, and after that, Derek just wanted revenge. It kept him up for nights on end while he planned how to get back at Dubois." Janet shrugged. "That's all I can tell you. He was a fool and now he's dead. Personally,

I don't think the world is a lesser place because he is gone. Quite the opposite, in fact."

Janet put the car in gear and drove off without so much as a goodbye, leaving Penny staring after her in disbelief.

The crew had made short work of dismantling the hay bales, and she followed Fischer as he went to investigate the line of yellowed grass beneath. She walked down the range to where the targets had stood. The ground in front was cut up slightly where missed arrows had thudded into the turf, but behind the spot where the colourful targets had stood Penny spotted a narrow area of fresh green grass. There had to have been a gap in the bales just behind the middle target. Obviously, no one would have been able to curve an arrow so it passed through the gap and the hedge beyond, possibly ending in the road behind.

"Look at this, Fish Face," Penny said, crouching to touch the verdant growth. The perimeter hedge was less than two feet away from her nose.

As a girl, she'd crawl into the hedges close to home and sit for hours reading, imagining the tunnel could lead her to the magic world in her book. She'd be lost for hours reading the adventures.

But as adventurous as she was when it came to her reading choices, she wasn't prepared to ruin her clothes in order to go scrabbling about in the hedgerow today. But she could see a small break in the branches where she could put her head in and take another look at the world that had once been so familiar and such a comfort to her. Fischer had no such qualms and dashed into the hedge, snuffling around happily.

"Don't go any further, Fischer. I don't want you running into the road."

She pulled out of the hedge just as her little dog came bursting onto the field twenty feet to her right. He came running over and dropped something at her feet. He looked up at her, smiling.

"What have you found there, little man?"

She picked up what she expected to be a scrap of litter, but realised it was a white cotton handkerchief.

"Well done, Fish Face," she said, giving him a treat. "Someone obviously lost this. Oh, look, it's monogrammed. Perhaps we can find the owner." She turned it over to read the letters stitched into one corner in dark blue thread.

A. D.

"I wonder who that could be?" She looked again from the archery range to where the marquee had stood. It looked as though someone crawling through the hedgerow had lost a handkerchief. Surely only a child would be crawling in there, though? But what child would own a monogrammed hankie?

"Come on, Fischer, we need to get back to work."

As Penny walked across the field with Fischer at her heel, she pulled out her phone and called John Monroe. Although the site had been searched, this might be a clue his team had missed.

The phone went to voice mail, so she left a message telling him what she'd found and that she'd keep hold of it for him.

Back at home that evening, Susie and the kids turned up out of the blue. Ellen and Billy had been pestering their mum about going to see Fischer, so after half an hour she'd relented, knowing she wouldn't get any peace until she did so. While Penny and Susie chatted over tea in the kitchen, the kids went off to the living room to read and play with Fischer. Penny always kept a number of children's books on hand for them.

They only stayed for an hour, so after she'd said goodbye, Penny went to tidy up. The books the kids had been reading were still lying on the floor. Ellen had left open anything and everything she could find about dinosaurs, while Billy had been reading a book about the Wild West. He'd left it open on a double page illustration of a Native American warrior. He was drawing back the bow and arrow, taking careful aim at a buffalo in the distance. She picked up the book and studied his posture. He was crouched down. One knee on the ground in a kneeling position.

EIGHT

There was plenty of time to spare when Penny pulled into the library parking spot at Holts End on Wednesday morning. She opened the van's double side doors and set up the small camping table and chair just outside. With Fischer curled up for his morning snooze under the camper, she sat down with her latest book and waited for her first customer of the day.

She was so engrossed in the murder mystery, she didn't hear the person behind her until they coughed. She jumped out of her chair and spun round. It was Tony Deacon.

"Tony, you startled me," she said with a gasp. "I was in another world. Can I help?"

He stepped up into the library and peered around the shelves. "Do you have anything that will make me feel less miserable? You know, cheer me up a bit?"

Penny studied the man more closely. He did look pretty wretched. She didn't know him at all well, but from what her friend Mr Kelly had told her, Tony Deacon was a highly emotional type. Unhappy and occasionally angry. She stepped up into the van, determined to find something that would be of benefit.

"I'm sure there's something here that can help. Can you tell me the reason you're feeling so low?"

Tony didn't seem to hear her, lost in his own world, staring at the books but not really seeing them. He obviously had a lot on his mind. She tried again.

"Can you tell me what's bothering you?"

He moved closer to the books and began to run his fingertip across their spines.

"I'm lonely," he said simply. "All the time."

Penny felt her heart contract. It made her sad to think someone felt so alone in the Downs. The residents always helped their neighbours, but sometimes their good natures and offers of help weren't enough. Penny felt Tony really needed to speak to a professional, but it wasn't her place to suggest it. He needed to reach that decision himself, or hear it from someone closer to him than she was.

"I miss my wife," Tony continued. "It's been nearly a year since she's been gone and it's not getting any easier. I just need something to take my mind off it and help me with the grief and... I've done things I regret. Things I'm not proud of, which I'll never be able to fix."

Penny recalled the incident Mr Kelly had told her about, about Tony losing his temper in the staff room at the school and smashing the cups. But judging by the look on his face, Tony Deacon wasn't talking about smashed crockery.

"I know this is only a small library, but if you've got anything at all that will help, I'd be grateful."

Penny took his desperate request seriously. It had obviously taken a lot of courage to come to her for help. It was beyond her job description as a mobile librarian to dispense emotional support of this kind, but maybe some of the leaflets in Winstoke library would have information about mental health care providers, or therapists that could offer him some support? She made a note to seek some out for next time. However, he was here now, and she'd do her very best to find something that could help in the short term.

Suddenly, Penny remembered a rather obscure book she'd added from the main library several months ago. It was by an American happiness guru and had never been checked out before. She told Sam and Emma she'd add it to the mobile library. Maybe someone in the outlying villages would be grateful for it. She couldn't think of a better recommendation for Tony, so moved to the right section, found it and showed it to him.

"I haven't read it, nor do I know anything about the author, but it certainly suggests it could be of some use to you."

She handed him the small book, then stepped out of the library. Even though she had a lot of sympathy for what Tony Deacon was going through, Penny felt uncomfortable sharing a small space with him.

Tony turned the book over and looked at the cover. But it was as though he couldn't see what he was looking at.

"I would do anything to have her back," he said softly. More to himself than to Penny.

He handed over his library card and Penny could see it had hardly been used in all the years he had owned it.

"Let me know if it's of help, Tony," she said as he wandered off. "Well, what do you think of that?" Penny said to the little dog who had come to stand by her side. But Fischer took no notice, staring after Deacon as he walked away. Perhaps he was making sure he left?

By the time Penny had a fresh pot of tea on her table and half a dozen happy library customers were on their way, clutching new, exciting books to read for the week, she'd practically forgotten all about Tony Deacon's visit.

As the morning sun began to heat up, her final customer of the morning stepped up, pulling her attention from the book she'd almost finished. He was someone she immediately recognised from around the villages, but had never spoken to. He appeared to be her age, or perhaps a little older, but she didn't remember him from school, so it was likely he was a newcomer. Although a newcomer in the Downs could be someone who'd lived in the area for years.

Easily remembered because he was a leather clad rocker with long hair graying at the temples. He had on a pure white tee shirt and tight black jeans. And come rain or shine, he always wore a black leather biker's jacket.

"Hi. Can I sign up to the library here? I'd love to grab a book if I can."

"Yes, of course, I can do that now for you," she climbed into the van. "I'll have to issue your card from the main library, but if I take your details now, you can borrow a book today."

She took an application form from a file and, pen poised, asked his name.

"Jack Stone. I live here in Holts End."

Penny filled in the form and asked Jack to sign it.

"You can pick up your card from me next week. So, is there anything you're specifically looking for or are you just browsing?"

Stone leaned in closer and glanced around nervously.

"I never learned to play the guitar," he said, shifting from foot to foot. "I don't know how the rumours started, but it's getting to be embarrassing having to say no every time I'm asked to play at the open mic night in town. People think I can play, you see. So, I need a book that can teach me the basics. I've had a guitar for several years, but I hardly know which end to blow into." He grinned at his joke and Penny laughed.

"I've several beginner music books. Let's see if there's something suitable."

Fischer jumped into the van and took his place on the driver's seat. He stood with his paws on the back of the seat and looked hopefully at Jack Stone, his tongue hanging out in his perpetual smile and his tail wagging furiously. The biker leaned over and scratched him behind the ears, eliciting a contented whine from the little dog, while Penny searched out some appropriate books.

"Did you go to the fair over the weekend?" she asked him.

"No, I was visiting a friend in the city. We had a few gigs to go to. That's what made me want to learn the guitar again."

"Sounds like a busy weekend," Penny said, handing over the books she dug out for him.

"It was. I love going to the city every so often, but I've gotta be honest. It's great to come back home."

He took the books and held them with a degree of reverence Penny was pleased to see.

"So you missed it all? That's a shame. It was a great weekend."

"Not quite all. I had to stop and take a call next to the field as I was riding back home. I'd just parked the bike when I heard a series of loud bangs. Couldn't work out what it was at first, then realised it was the war re-enactment. Then I spied someone crawling through the hedge with what looked like an arrow in his hand. I couldn't work out if he was from the society or not? Did they even have bows and arrows in the civil war? History is not my strong suit."

"I've got books on the subject, if you're interested?" Penny said, smiling.

Stone held up his music books.

"These will do for now. No, actually, do you have any song books? Something that will help me learn a simple tune?"

"I do," she said, removing the books. He took the Dolly Parton one, overlooking the Rolling Stones and the Beatles, and tucked it in his jacket.

"You're sworn to secrecy like a doctor or solicitor, yes? A librarian isn't allowed to discuss what books a patron takes out, right?" He asked, a bit sheepishly.

"Absolutely. It's the librarian's code. I shall not tell a soul."

Jack Stone thanked her for her help and she wished him luck with his lessons. As soon as he left, Penny began to pack away, her mind turning over what he'd told her about someone crawling through the hedge with an arrow in their hand.

Penny had seen Alan Dubois looking highly suspicious around the back of the food marquee, and he'd had a grass stain on one knee of his trousers. An image of the Native American warrior came into her mind. And then there was the monogrammed handkerchief that her clever little dog had found. Alan always carried one.

She shut the camper van doors and jumped into the driver's seat.

"A. D. It's definitely a clue, Fischer."

Fischer barked once, agreeing with her.

She was working on the investigation without consciously planning to, and every clue was bringing her closer to the killer. She only hoped she wasn't adding two and two and making five.

NINE

After a good walk for Fischer, Penny and her little companion walked to the Pot and Kettle to meet Susie for lunch. This was a welcome and much anticipated treat for Wednesday afternoon. Although it wasn't set in stone, it was a frequent, if not regular, event.

As they approached, she saw Susie's car was already parked outside. A quick check of the time and Penny was satisfied she wasn't running late.

The little bell above the door tinkled as they entered and she waved to the owner, who immediately went to get a bowl of water for Fischer. He was one of the cafe's favourite patrons. She approached the table in the bay window, where Susie was intently studying the menu. Her friend looked up and smiled as Penny said hello and Fischer jumped up for an ear scratch.

"Hi. Sorry, I was miles away. I've ordered a pot of English Breakfast tea for us both. Hope that's okay?"

"Just what I need. Thanks, Susie."

At that moment, the waitress brought a tray with a china pot for two, along with matching cups and saucers. She laid them efficiently on the table, along with the milk jug and sugar bowl, but Penny couldn't help notice her nervous glances toward the table tucked into the corner. Partially hidden by the service counter and the wrought iron spiral staircase that led up to the mezzanine seating area.

Penny followed her gaze and recognised the patron. Alan Dubois was slowly eating a slice of Victoria sponge cake. As he finished each mouthful, he let out a sigh, then took another. Eating with care and deliberation.

Penny noticed the waiting staff, two young women from the village, were watching his every move. But their anxiousness was nothing compared to the chefs and the owner, who were peering out from behind the kitchen door.

"I'm not pushed for time, but I think I'll just have a sandwich," Susie said, pouring tea for them both.

Penny was still mesmerised by Alan Dubois, particularly when he pulled out a white handkerchief to dab his mouth. She strained forward to see if she could spot a monogram.

"Penny, are you here? Or am I having lunch on my own?"

"Sorry, Susie. What were you saying?"

"My boss has got me on the death at the fair story. I don't suppose you got any juice morsels from John Monroe that you can pass on, did you?"

"Not really. I told him what you'd found out about Alan Dubois, but he doesn't give out information about ongoing investigations, Susie, you know that."

Susie sighed. The waitress came over and they both ordered sandwiches and a bowl of French fries to share. When she'd gone, Penny leaned forward.

"I found something earlier at the sports field. I've left a message for John about it, but he hasn't called back. Don't use what I tell you. I'm not sure I should be telling anyone."

"I won't say a word."

"You're a reporter, Susie. Words are your living."

"True. But I promise I'll sit on the information until I can officially use it. Go on."

"I found a clue. A monogrammed handkerchief. Well, Fischer found it actually. In the hedge. It had the initials A. D. embroidered on one corner." Penny nodded her head toward the corner table.

"Who else could it belong to? He thinks he's superior with his airs and graces, but he doesn't fool me. It's all an act. He's as common as the rest of us."

"Speak for yourself," Penny said in mock admonishment.

Susie smiled, but glanced quizzically over at Alan Dubois, who was sipping his tea with his little finger stuck up in the air.

"I also spoke to Janet Cotton," Penny continued after their food had arrived. "Between you and me, she is far from sorry her husband is dead. It's obvious their marriage was not a happy one."

"Too many people know what an unhappy relationship is like," Susie replied, her eyes darkening with sorrow.

Penny really felt for her friend. She'd been happily married right up to the point when she'd discovered her husband had been having an affair. It had been a gut-wrenching shock for Susie when he'd left. In complete contrast, her own relationship had been devoid of any real affection for so long it had been a relief when it ended.

"But is being unhappy in a marriage enough to drive someone to murder?" Susie asked.

"It's happened many times. But, at the very least, it's grounds for divorce," Penny said, then instantly regretted it.

Susie sensed Penny's discomfort and shook her head.

"Don't worry, I'm doing fine. Honestly. We can't dwell on these things forever, and I can't have you skirting around words and subjects just because you think you might upset me." Susie took a sip of her tea. "Thank you for the other night, by the way. Friendly company was just what I needed. I know I get miserable about James sometimes, but really I know we are all better off with the way things worked out. As long as the children have contact with their father and they know how much we both love them, everything is fine. James dotes on the children and that's all I need to make me happy. And I know how much they mean to you too, Penny. You should hear the way they talk about you. They love visiting you and Fischer. You always have something fun and interesting for them to do. Actually, I've just remembered. Billy was asking if he could borrow that book about the Wild West? We could pop in and pick it up one day when we're passing."

Penny said, of course, then glanced back at Alan Dubois. He didn't look like an archer. He looked for all the world like he'd always been a food critic.

"Hang on, Susie. I'm just going to have a quick word with our resident food critic."

"Mr Dubois," Penny said. "I thought it was you. I hope I'm not intruding?" Then, without giving him a chance to answer, she fixed a friendly smile on her face and plunged on. "What brings you to the Pot and Kettle? I thought fancy restaurants were more your style?"

Dubois looked up at Penny, dabbing the corner of his mouth with his handkerchief. He was eying her as he would a morsel of food, something to be considered at length before passing comment.

Penny found his manner aloof and condescending, but maintained her smile, unwavering under his scrutiny. Fischer stood just behind her, pressed tight against her ankle, peering at the food critic with suspicion.

Finally, after a deep breath, Dubois deigned to speak.

"I will eat anywhere that serves good food."

"Well, you've certainly come to the right place today. Are you planning on doing a write up?"

"I only review the establishments that invite me. Today, I am here for a simple lunch break. It doesn't matter whether it's good or bad, I won't be writing about it either way. But for your information, it is excellent. And that is an Alan Dubois review you can have for free."

"Oh, so if you only review by invitation, Derek Cotton must have invited you to Bistro 23?"

Dubois gave Penny a suspicious look. He reminded her of a hawk with his beak-like nose and small, piercing, almost black eyes.

"He did. The meal was excellent. Top class, in fact. Cooked to perfection and stylishly presented without being ostentatious. I was composing an exemplary review for the bistro, but it was spoiled by the man himself. He was a constant pest with his fawning and fussing. Hovering over me like a vulture. He made the whole experience tedious and irritating. Had it not been for him, I would have scored the establishment four chefs hats. As it was, I reduced it to one."

This was news to Penny. She'd assumed, as many others who had read the review had, that it was down to the food rather than the over obsequiousness of Derek Cotton that had caused Dubois to score the bistro so poorly. But Alan Dubois wasn't finished.

"The final straw came when he got in the way of the waitress, causing her to fumble a plate. She was so dexterous and skilful that she managed to keep hold of the plate with limited spillage, but Cotton had the temerity to scold her rather than apologise for his mistake. The poor child was flushed with shame and embarrassment. At that moment, I knew he was not getting a positive review from me. Good waiting staff are as important to a restaurant as a good chef, but at Bistro 23, they were all at the mercy of a hopeless and tyrannical owner. He was a nuisance and my review clearly stated it was the owner, not the chef, nor the staff, who was at fault."

That wasn't quite how Penny remembered it, but she wasn't going to argue with him.

"And then he took you to court for it."

"He did. In an attempt to sue me for loss of earnings as a result of my review. He still blamed the waitress, saying I'd marked down the service when I was supposed to be there to sample the food. But what he didn't understand was that they are all part of the experience of good dining. It doesn't have to be fancy, or experimental, or ground breaking. I've seen enough seaweed foam and vegetable jus that tasted of nothing more than cabbage water to be singularly unimpressed with pompous presentation. A well cooked meal is a pleasure as old as time, and a welcoming, courteous environment has always been foods' best seasoning."

Penny could hear the writer coming out of Dubois as he pontificated at length, expounding on a topic he was overly familiar with. She thought she could also sense his growing ease in her company.

"Were you concerned he was suing you?"

"Not enough to kill the man," Dubois said, looking up at her with cold eyes. "We all know of your reputation, Miss Finch. If there's a mystery to be solved, then you're all over it like brown sauce on a bacon sandwich." Penny winced at the analogy. "No, Miss Finch, I didn't kill Derek Cotton. As odious as the man was, he couldn't drive me to such appalling behaviour, because I simply don't care enough about him."

Dubois reached down to touch Fischer but the little dog moved away, turned his back and lifted his nose in the air. Dubois withdrew his hand.

"I have had many legal threats made against me. And even more death threats. I've been doing this job for far too long to take any of them seriously. I have insurance against being sued, but I am very careful as well as being honest in what I write. So many restaurateurs want to challenge Alan Dubois. They think if they can impress me, they will receive a boost to their business. That is what Cotton thought, but he made the whole dining experience a chore. However, I did feel sympathy for the man. I am not a monster. He was struggling to keep his business afloat, and he blamed the Dubois' review for almost finishing him off. But, my readers are just as likely to visit an establishment that has received a bad review as a good one. My readers don't want to know just what Dubois enjoyed, they want to know what Dubois disliked."

Penny thought how odd it was that Alan Dubois kept referring to himself in the third person. It was an unsettling feeling. Susie came over then, and Penny immediately felt guilty for leaving her friend alone.

"Why don't you leave Mr Dubois to his lunch, Penny?" Susie said, putting a friendly hand on the critic's arm and apologising. As she pulled away, she knocked his handkerchief off the table and onto the floor. Dubois stooped to pick it up, but Susie was faster. "I do apologise," she said, lifting the hankie and quickly showing Penny both sides. It was completely plain.

"Here you are. I would have thought a man of your standing would have a monogrammed handkerchief," she said.

Dubois rolled his eyes and scoffed.

"Not I. How utterly bourgeois."

"Well, thank you for your time, Mr Dubois. I'll leave you in peace to finish your lunch," Penny said.

Once seated, Susie and Penny made short work of the remaining food.

"No monogram," Susie said. "So what now?"

"Now, I need to go or I'll be late back to the library. I'll have my regular customers staging a revolt if I don't open on time. It will make the civil war look like a minor skirmish."

Penny was opening the van doors just as the first customers arrived. Fischer greeted everyone in turn, shaking hands and rolling over for treats. The little dog was one of the reasons the library had so many customers.

As Penny greeted everyone one at a time, chatting about their favourite books and recommending new reads, her mind wandered. She thought of Alan Dubois. As a bronze medal winning archer, he was certainly more than capable of shooting the arrow that had killed Derek Cotton, but from what she'd heard about his reputation and his own admission in the cafe earlier, he was far too aloof and indifferent to go to the trouble of murder. He didn't seem worried that his review had upset Derek, nor that it had resulted in a court case. Penny also had to conclude it was unlikely to have been his handkerchief Fischer had found in the hedge. Although she couldn't come up with anyone else who shared his initials.

As she was mulling over potential suspects, she considered Derek's wife. She'd been stuck in a loveless marriage, but for how long? It was impossible to know. Maybe they had never been in love at all, but neither had had the courage to break off the relationship before it was too late and they were married.

Her thoughts drifted to Edward. How easily she could have made the same mistake. But for all the tragedy and pain of a loveless marriage, could Mrs Cotton really have committed murder to be free? She struck Penny as a woman who would just walk out. But then again, she had mentioned huge debts that, as Derek's wife, she would be liable for.

The more Penny thought, the more questions she had. She couldn't shake from her mind the image of Derek Cotton lying in the field with an arrow sticking out of his neck. No one had seen who'd made the shot and few could have hit that small a target from such a distance.

She was saved from the grizzly image by the excited yapping of Fischer greeting his friends Gatsby and Daisy, the young black Labradors. Mr Sheridan, the dog's owner, called out a cheerful hello as he sauntered up to the library, leaving

Fischer and his pooches to play chase happily under and around the van.

"I didn't know if I was going to make it this week. Gatsby and Daisy are growing so fast and have so much energy, they could have walked me around Sugar Hill half a dozen times today. I completely lost track of time."

Penny was always glad to see Mr Sheridan and the dogs. The week wouldn't be the same without their visit.

"I've no idea what book to get this week. To be honest, I'm so worn out I'll probably be fast asleep in my armchair before I've read a chapter."

"In that case, I think I might have just the thing," Penny said, stepping inside the camper and grabbing a book from the crime section. "Why not try this? Deadly Anniversaries. It's a collection of stories from Crime Fiction's top authors. Long enough to be satisfying, but short enough that you can read a page or two and be engaged enough before you fall asleep."

Mr Sheridan took the book and turned it over, stifling a yawn as he read the blurb. "There's some of my favourite authors in here. It's perfect. Thank you, Penny, he said. He fished out his library card and handed it over. With the book officially checked out, he said goodbye and left with his dogs walking to heel.

Penny turned back and spied a familiar car parked just behind the van. She smiled. It was John Monroe.

"Hello, Penny. I didn't want to disturb you while you were with a customer."

"Thank you," she replied, surreptitiously checking her reflection in the van's side mirrors and trying to smooth her unruly hair without appearing to. "I take it you've not come all the way to Thistle Grange to pick up a book?"

Monroe smiled and shook his head.

"And you'd be right. I got your message about the handkerchief. Thank you. Do you have it with you?"

"Yes, I left it in the van so I'd remember to drop it in when I was next in town." She stepped up into the van and retrieved the cleaned lunch box she'd stored the hankie in and handed it over.

She thought it a little strange that John Monroe had travelled all the way over to Thistle Grange to pick it up. Maybe there was something else on his mind? She sensed he was hesitating, as though he had an additional question to ask her.

"Can I help with anything else? A book? Or perhaps a cup of tea?"

Penny sensed Monroe was happy to stay and chat, so put the kettle on to boil and retrieved a second cup from the van, while he took a seat at her little table.

"I took the official statement from Tony Deacon this morning," Monroe told her. "He said he was at the archery range the whole time. He was collecting arrows just before you discovered the body and didn't see anyone near the bows. But he was concentrating on his task and wasn't really looking. All the bows are accounted for, so nobody took one away.

It's a complete mystery at the moment. I have no idea who could have shot that arrow."

"Could it have been Deacon himself?" Penny asked.

"Not from where he was standing. The bows used for the fair just aren't that powerful. The target was hard enough to hit as it was, and it was the size of a barn door. I honestly don't believe Deacon could have hit such a small target as Derek Cotton's neck from that distance. It was a crack shot."

He was interrupted by the ringing of his phone. He fished it from his pocket and looked at the screen with a sigh.

"Work. I am sorry, I have to go. Thanks for this," he added, holding up the lunch box containing the hankie. "I'll be in touch soon."

He gave her a wave as he drove away. They seemed to be good at snatching a few minutes of company and conversation here and there, but nothing more. She really needed to find time to tell him what she'd learned so far, even if it didn't amount to very much.

TEN

Although every day in Hampsworthy Downs was a pleasure, Penny enjoyed Thursdays more than any other day. She could take a little longer in bed reading her book, as she was based in her own village of Cherrytree Downs for the first half, so her drive to work was the shortest of the whole week. Then after the morning was over, she would head to the main library in Winstoke to re-stock with new books for the following week and catch up with her colleagues Sam and Emma.

After waking a full hour before her alarm went off, Penny enjoyed a lazy lie in, finishing off the mystery she'd begun a few days before. When the alarm finally sounded, she threw off the covers and leapt out of bed. Swiftly followed by a happy, tail thumping little dog, who knew breakfast and a joyous sniff around the back garden was imminent.

As much as she enjoyed the few extra minutes in bed, she didn't resent having to get up for work. Even on the coldest days, when the frost was making decorative patterns on the outside of her window. Being the only mobile librarian in the area, her job wasn't simply a means to pay the bills, it was a passion.

Grabbing the keys from the bowl on the hall table, she looked down at Fischer, who was holding his lead in his mouth ready to go, and smiled. He really was the brightest little dog. There had been a shower in the night and the morning sun was glinting off the damp roof tops as the two of them jumped into the van. Fischer sat upright, excited for the journey to come.

"It's Thursday, I'm afraid, Fish Face," Penny said as she parked a few minutes later. "But we're going to town this afternoon, so you've got a long ride to look forward to."

Not far from where she'd parked, Penny could see local builder Terry Stokes standing in front of the old police house. He was picking away at the pointing between the old red bricks with a small metal tool, probing and testing before making notes in a small book. The short, stubby pencil was dwarfed by his huge calloused hands. A pair of half-moon spectacles sat on the end of his bulbous nose.

The police house was vacant now the old village bobby, PC Humphrey Bolton, had retired. She'd heard it would be put up for sale and as Terry was obviously working on the old property, it was possible he knew more. She glanced at her watch and found it was a few minutes before she was due to open, so decided to wander over for a chat to see what she could find out. Fischer stayed to heel as she crossed the road.

"Morning, Terry," she said. "Making an early start, I see."

"Finch," he said, snatching off his glasses. "Haven't you got work to do?"

Penny smiled, ignoring Stokes' bad tempered tone. He was never in a good mood and was always rude. "I'm based here in the village today."

Terry rolled his eyes.

"So I'll have you bothering me all day, I suppose?"

"I'll be far too busy to bother you once I open, Terry. And I'm in town this afternoon, so don't worry. You're working on the police house?"

Stokes just looked at her as though she were an imbecile. "Obviously."

"So is it for the next village bobby, or has it been sold?"

"Not that it's any of your business, but I have a work order from the police to check the property and carry out any maintenance work that needs doing. That's as far as it goes. I don't ask questions, only that they pay on time."

He looked the old house up and down and Penny could see admiration in his eyes.

"It just needs a bit of re-pointing and a couple of floor boards are loose upstairs, but she's in good shape for her age. She's a fine old house."

"Do you know when the next owner will be moving in?"

"Never if you don't leave me alone to get on with the work," he replied grumpily.

Penny grinned.

"Okay, well, it's been great chatting with you, Terry. Have a good day."

Penny and Fischer wandered back to the library and opened up.

The morning flew by with eager customers arriving at regular intervals. No sooner had one left another arrived. They took time perusing the books, giving Fischer lots of attention and treats and chatting. But there was one topic on almost everyone's lips. The local murder.

Talk of the death had almost everyone gravitating to the library's crime section. It had already been borrowed from heavily during the week and by the end of her Thursday morning session, it was completely emptied of books. From Agatha Christie to P. D. James and everything in between, every last book was out on loan. She made a note to increase her stock of mysteries for the following week. Obviously there were more than a few amateur sleuths in Hampsworthy Downs hoping to solve the case.

Driving along the hedge lined country roads was a treat for Fischer. He was sat up alert and smiling, looking out of the van's window. Penny rather envied her little dog, there was much to see during the journey, from the wildflowers in the meadows, the sheep and cows grazing in the fields, to the wild creatures, such as the rabbits and hares hopping from the grassy areas to the various copse' where they could shelter unseen from the sharp eyes of the birds of prey above. Yet, she had to concentrate on the road while her furry companion could admire the beautiful countryside rolling by.

Winstoke town was thriving when Penny pulled up across the road from the main library. The old castle on the high ground was looking dramatic against the afternoon sky, framed by white fluffy clouds hanging in a sweep of bright blue. The castle ruin had been saved from total collapse by the people of the town and the surrounding villages and was no longer in danger of crumbling. The broken towers continued their watch over the market town as they had done for centuries. Preserved by the descendants of those they had once protected.

Carrying boxes of books back and forth between the van and the library was the most strenuous work of the week for Penny. Several trips were required to fully swap the current stock for a fresh selection. Once she'd completed the job, she locked the van doors and joined her colleagues, Sam and Emma, who'd been entertaining Fischer while she was busy.

No Thursday afternoon would be complete without a pot of tea and a plate of assorted biscuits. The storyteller had just finished her session, and the children were leaving the library, all excited as they marched out in pairs with tales of ancient kings and queens fresh in their imaginations.

"No storyteller next week," Emma said. "She's on holiday."

"I could do with a holiday," Sam said. "Somewhere with sea and sunshine and maybe an adventure or two."

"What, and leave all this behind?" Emma said, encompassing the entire library with a wide sweep of her arm.

"This was almost as good as a week off." Penny pulled a book from her bag and dropped it on the counter. "I just finished it this morning. Murder, mystery, mayhem and adventure on the French Riviera."

Emma snatched the book from the counter and turned it over to read the blurb.

"That sounds really good. Here Sam, why don't you take it? You need a holiday more than I do." She turned to Penny. "He's been distracted all week, and at the fair he was standing staring into space for so long I thought he'd been hypnotised. It was only the shots from the muskets that brought him back to the present."

"I wasn't staring into space," Sam said, taking the book. "I was watching Linda Green the jam lady."

"Why? What was she doing?" Penny asked.

"Sneaking round the back of the food marquee. I didn't think there was any space back there being right up against the hedge. I just wondered what she was doing, that's all."

"When was that, Sam? Can you remember?" Penny asked, feeling a frisson of excitement run up her spine.

Sam thought about it for a minute.

"I'm not sure. But she reappeared just when Derek Cotton was found. You don't think she had something to do with it, do you?"

It actually was something Penny had briefly considered. She'd overheard Linda and Derek talking less than half an hour before his death, and there was clearly no love lost between them. Accusations of stealing recipes had been bandied about. Penny wouldn't have minded anyone taking one of her recipes, in fact she'd gladly write them out for whoever wanted them, but maybe things were different in a professional kitchen where a chef's dishes were as unique as a signature and recipes were a jealously guarded secret.

It was something she needed to look into further, and there was no time like the present.

After saying goodbye to her colleagues, Penny drove out of Winstoke, but instead of taking the country road that would take her to Rowan Downs and then on to her home village, she went out onto the duel carriageway.

Linda Green had mentioned she was getting a burger van very soon, and this was to be her pitch. While it had only been five days, Penny hoped Linda was already up and running. She drove within the speed limit, being overtaken by cars in the outside lane, while she scanned ahead for a food van. She soon spotted it. A large Union Jack flying above the small fast food takeaway showed off its location to those on the road who might otherwise have sped by before noticing it was there.

Penny pulled into the lay-by and turned off the engine. A narrow strip of overgrown weed filled grass with a couple of silver birch trees divided the parking spot from the main road, but it was dreadfully noisy with cars and lorries constantly rumbling past.

Fischer had his paws on the passenger side window, taking in the new scenery. It was a route Penny very seldom took, preferring the quiet country roads, so it was all quite new and interesting for the little dog.

"It's better if I leave you here, Fish Face," Penny said as she slipped out of the van, shutting Fischer safely inside.

The smell of frying meat assaulted Penny's nose as she approached, causing her stomach to flip in revolt. She made an effort to breathe through her mouth and walked over.

"Hi Linda, you've got your new van. Congratulations."

Linda glanced at Penny a little suspiciously but couldn't help the proud look on her face at having finally got her own business. It was a reconditioned horse box that remarkably housed all the fixtures and fittings of a working kitchen.

"Yes, I got it. It's not the Ritz, but it's all mine and will do until I can get back on my feet. So, what can I get you?"

Penny peered inside and saw a single box of supermarket tea bags and a tin of instant coffee granules. She would have been happy to have a cup of tea, but the commercial water boiler was sitting adjacent to the hot plate and she could see it had already been splattered with meat fat.

She could sense Linda was getting a bit irritated with her taking so long to come to a simple decision. She was used to truck drivers ordering quickly. She spotted a small fridge filled with pop and water bottles. That seemed like a safe choice.

"A bottle of water, please," she said, digging out her purse and putting the right change on the counter. "Isn't it awful what happened to Derek Cotton at the fair? Did you see what happened?"

"I've already told the police everything. I saw nothing," Linda said, folding her arms and leaning against the edge of the serving hatch. "That detective inspector is pretty dishy, though, don't you think? I'd serve him up something tasty given half the chance."

"Did you tell him you were hiding behind the food marquee moments before Cotton was shot with that arrow?"

"I wasn't hiding," Linda bristled. "I was with someone."

"Anyone I know?" Penny said with a smile. The quip about John Monroe had irked her, but she needed to keep Linda onside and not provoke her if she was going to get the information she sought.

"I was with Alan Dubois, if you must know."

Penny had seen Dubois behind the large tent, but she couldn't picture him and Linda together in that way. The woman must mean something else.

"What were you doing there?"

"He asked me for a chat in private, away from the others in the tent. I thought he was going to ask me about my food, or about my work at Bistro 23. I was the chef there when he wrote his review. But he didn't ask about any of that. He told me he loved me. That he's been plucking up the courage to tell me for months. I tell you, I was so surprised I nearly fell in the hedge. But then he went and spoiled it by saying I was 'earthy.' By that he meant common, I know. I may very well be, but he is short and rude." Linda curled her hair around a finger and her face took on a coquettish look as she reminisced. Penny's mouth had fallen open at the revelation and she couldn't seem to close it. Linda went on. "He is cute, though, in a funny sort of way. Clumsy talking. Shy even, but his writing is pure poetry and clever. I'm not so common that I don't read proper news and restaurant reviews."

Penny was struggling to put her thoughts into words. Green was unabashed and forward, sharing every little detail, some of which should have been kept quiet. It was obvious Linda had been desperate to tell someone since it happened, and as she was there at the right time, she'd chosen Penny.

Penny didn't have much of a silence to fill as Linda hardly took a breath now she was in her stride.

"And I think I love him, too. But we're so different. He thinks I'm common and I think he's a pompous snob. He's too short and likes really elaborate food, where I like straight forward cooking, simple and delicious. I can cook all the fancy French stuff and I'm good at it, but down to earth British meals are what I like best. It's honest."

"Right," Penny said, nodding. "So it was nothing more than a coincidence you were just having a chat when Derek was killed?"

"A chat?" Linda scoffed. "He proposed to me."

"He proposed?" Penny managed to squeak, unscrewing the cap off her water and taking a deep drink. She wished it was something a bit stronger. She didn't know how many more revelations she could take.

"That's right. Down on one knee and everything. Then he said it had to be a secret! I mean, how was that supposed to work? Obviously, he was ashamed. Anyway, I was about to turn him down when there were those loud bangs, so I went to see what was going on. And that's all I know."

For once, Penny couldn't think of anything to say. She spotted a small stack of individually wrapped carrot cake slices on the counter.

"Did you make these? They look delicious. I don't suppose many of the truckers go for it though, do they?"

"You'd be surprised. Sitting and driving all day, they don't get much exercise and are looking for some more healthy alternatives. That carrot cake, my own recipe by the way, is a very tasty treat with far fewer calories than any normal piece of fruit cake. No sugar, all natural sweetness. That's how I lost all my extra weight. You should try it," she added, looking Penny up and down.

Penny stared at her, dumbfounded. No one had ever made snide comments about her weight. Well, not to her face, at least. Actually strike that, she thought, one person had. Her former fiancé. But she wasn›t going to think about Edward. It was Linda Green who had no filter. She just blurted out whatever came into her mind, no matter how tactless or hurtful it sounded. Penny was failing to understand what Alan Dubois saw in her. She was undoubtedly pretty, but she was also very brassy. Perhaps it was the food? Penny immediately felt guilty for her uncharitable thoughts. Linda could very well be a different person when she was with Alan.

"Is that all you want?" Linda suddenly barked at her. "Just the water?"

"How much for a piece of carrot cake?"

"A pound."

Penny handed over the coin and dropped the cake in her bag. She was about to say goodbye, but Linda had turned her back and was already scrolling through her phone.

"Down on one knee, Fischer," Penny said as she climbed into the van. "So that must be how Dubois picked up the grass stain. So perhaps it wasn't him who shot the arrow. But who else could have hit Derek Cotton from such a distance?"

Just as she was about to set off, her phone rang. It was John Monroe. She turned off the engine and answered the call.

ELEVEN

Although the heavy traffic was rumbling by just a few feet to her right, inside the camper van, surrounded by books, she was isolated from the worst of the noise. She climbed into the back as she answered the call.

"Hello, John," she said, making herself comfortable on the little camping chair she kept in the back. Fischer jumped up on her knee, tail wagging furiously as though he knew who the caller was. "Can I help with something?"

"Actually, it's a social call. Not that I have much time off these days, but I could do with a break. I wanted to ask if you're still going to the pub quiz tonight?"

Penny couldn't help the grin that spread across her face, elated at the thought of being able to spend some quality time with John.

"Yes, I'm still going. I wouldn't miss it. Hopefully, we can give the other teams a run for their money."

"I've been brushing up on my royal history. Maybe my efforts will be worth a point or two?"

"Fingers crossed. I'll see you at the pub later, then."

"You will. Bye for now, Penny."

The Thursday night pub quiz had become a regular event for Penny, Susie, and their new team mate John Monroe, and they always made time to attend. But, after all this time playing together as a unit, their combined knowledge and copious amounts of revising, their team, Agatha Quiztee, still couldn't get a win over their closest rivals, Universally Challenged.

"Maybe tonight is the night. What do you think, Fischer?" Penny said, scrabbling over to the driver's seat and starting the engine.

———•———

After a light snack to stave off her hunger pangs, but wouldn't ruin her appetite for the food which always accompanied quiz night at the Pig and Whistle, Penny had a quick shower and after feeding Fischer, they both headed out for the evening.

The walk through the village was relaxing and Penny stopped to say hello and have a quick chat to a few neighbours who were out and about, enjoying the pleasant summer evening. A quick lap of the duck pond and a visit to the village green for Fischer, then they made a beeline for the pub.

Penny was greeted by the familiar creak of the ancient timber door on its iron hinges as she pushed it open, immediately followed by a welcome blast of happy chatter from the patrons at the bar. The old flagstone floor had felt the feet of a thousand locals stretching all the way back to the doomsday book. There was a familiar comfort in an old building that had existed for so long, and coming here Penny always felt as though she were both part of a history and of a future that was still being written.

Susie was at the bar and turned to greet her as the door closed. She had a glass of white wine in each hand and a broad smile on her face.

"I took the liberty of getting a round in," she said, handing the glass over and crouching down to give Fischer a hug.

"Thank you, Susie," Penny said, tapping glasses with her friend. "Cheers."

They glanced round the pub and found their usual table by the unlit fire was free, so sat down while Fischer lay underneath to watch the world go by from floor level.

"Where are the children tonight?"

"With their grandparents, James' parents. They are going to a little bed and breakfast by the seaside for a few days. Fish and chips, ice cream, candy floss and the fairground. I almost wish I was going with them. Mind you, it does mean I can sleep in on Saturday and Sunday mornings."

"You know, you can always come for a long morning walk across Sugar Hill with Fischer and me. We can call for you at about sixty-thirty."

"Ha! You won't get an answer. So, where's our history expert? Maybe we can get him to arrest the opposition to give us a decent shot at first place for a change."

Penny laughed.

"I'll leave you to suggest that. Don't worry, he called me earlier. He'll be here. Although I doubt he'll be up for making wrongful arrests. It's his night off."

"Then we're doomed," Susie said, with a grin. She raised her glass. "To defeat. Again."

Penny clinked glasses and downed the last mouthful of her wine. She glanced at the door as it opened. She was hoping it would be John, but it was a member of the rival team. He was a short bald man with a bulbous nose he always joked he'd pinched from a kid's TV character. He was friendly, but slightly awkward and without much confidence. Penny always noticed he made himself the butt of the joke before someone else could. He gave Penny a nod when he saw her watching and she smiled and nodded back.

"It's my round, Susie. Same again?"

On her way back from the bar, Penny spotted Alan Dubois and Linda Green at a cozy table in the corner. They were sharing a bag of cheese and onion crisps. Dubois held one up to the light, then carefully put it in his mouth and immediately pulled a face. He clearly didn't like the flavour. Linda laughed raucously, the sound filling the pub.

Susie had also seen them and mouthed 'wow,' to Penny when she returned to their table. "Linda Green and Alan Dubois? I would never have put those two together."

"It looks like they're on a date. They look really happy."

Suddenly, Alan Dubois stood up and cleared his throat.

"Everyone, I have an announcement."

The patrons turned and there was silence as Alan took Linda's hand and got down on one knee.

"Linda, I first fell in love with your food." There were a few chuckles throughout the room at this admission. "Then I fell in love with you. Will you do me the honor of becoming my wife?"

Linda grinned and blushed slightly. She thumped him playfully on his shoulder. His glasses shifted, but he managed to stay upright.

"Of course I'll marry you." She pulled him to his feet and kissed him deeply.

The pub erupted in cheering and applause. Penny and Susie stood and joined in. Fischer was also on his feet and woofing in excitement. Then John Monroe walked in.

"Did I miss something?" He said loudly over the hubbub.

"Hey, that might be you two one day," Susie said.

"What?" Penny said, glaring at her friend.

"What?" she replied, taking a sip of wine, her eyes dancing mischievously over the rim.

"I'll just go and get a pint," Monroe said, shooting Susie a confused look.

Penny groaned. He'd heard what Susie had said, too.

"Don't you dare do that again, Susie. I mean it."

"I was only having a bit of fun. I was caught up in the moment, that's all."

"I know. But, no more, okay?"

Monroe returned with a pint of Guinness just as the quiz was starting.

"You're cutting it a bit fine tonight, John," Susie said. "We weren't sure if you'd make it."

"Work. I got caught up in a few things that needed my attention. But I certainly wasn't going to let all my revision be for nothing. Besides, it's the highlight of my week." He glanced at Penny and smiled. "Shall I write the answers this time?"

The first round was current affairs and was conducted in all seriousness as the teams quietly conferred. Penny leaned forward over the answer sheet, speaking softly to Monroe. They settled on ten answers for round one, confident they'd got them all right.

As they moved into round two, Penny was aware of just how close she and John were. She'd had butterflies of excitement in her stomach since she'd arrived, but now they were kicking up a storm. He smelled of fresh soap and sandalwood, a seductive combination. She ached to reach out and touch him, but instead lifted her glass and took a healthy swallow of wine.

"Another round?" Susie asked, making Penny jump slightly. She'd almost forgotten she was there.

"Yes," John said. "A picture round, I think."

"I meant, do you want another drink from the bar?"

Both Penny and Monroe declined, so Susie went for herself.

"So," Penny said. "It appears that Linda Green and Alan Dubois were both at the rear of the food marquee together when Derek Cotton was shot."

John raised an eyebrow.

"And you know this how, Miss Finch? No, don't tell me. You were sleuthing again?"

Penny shrugged and grinned.

"You know me. I just can't seem to help myself."

"Yes, I've come to realise that. What were they doing, if it's not too personal a question? Or don't I want to know?"

"He was proposing to her. And he's just done it again in here. Making it official and public. That's what we were all clapping for when you came in."

"I see. That makes then one another's alibi."

"Yes, I suppose it does. Do you think it was them?"

Monroe shook his head.

"No, not now. They were persons of interest initially, but I've ruled them out. We're looking into another potential suspect."

Penny leaned closer.

"Really? Someone new to the investigation?"

John laughed.

"As much as I find your interest and curiosity endearing, Penny, you know I can't answer any of your questions."

Penny felt a warm glow over her entire body at John's words, and a rush of heat suffuse her face. She was acting like a teenager in the first throws of an infatuation, but she couldn't help it, her body was reacting entirely of its own volition and she could no more stop it than turn back the tides. She could see John felt it too as the laughter died and his eyes darkened with desire. She'd never know what could have happened next as Susie returned from the bar.

"TV and film round next," she said, putting a half pint glass of lime and lemonade on the table. "I like this round. Although I'd like it more if I knew all the answers."

As the pub quiz entered its final round, the three of them were increasingly confident about their chances. They went through a final check and, apart from two or three, they thought they'd got the answers right.

With the announcement from the pub landlord, the quiz was finished. Monroe took their answer sheet to the next table and swapped with that team for marking. As the correct answers were called out, the pub was filled with varying groans, cheers and laughter. Monroe collected their sheet and put it on the table with a large grin at Penny and Susie.

"That's a good score," Susie said. "We don't often see a winning score higher than that. I think we have a real chance of coming first this week."

Penny smiled and nodded, but her concentration and interest in the quiz had died away. She had other things on her mind.

Eventually, with the landlord in receipt of the final numbers, he announced the scores in reverse order. A pair of young guys in the corner, who'd only come out for a beer and decided to join in for a laugh, calling their team 'and the winners are,' came last with a derisory total. They cheered their score, standing to take an exaggerated bow before bouncing to the bar for another pint before closing time.

"In third place," the landlord called out, "Artificial Intelligence. Second place goes to Agatha Quiztee. Meaning tonight's winners are once again, but only by two points, Universally Challenged. Give them a round of applause, ladies and gentleman."

"Two points!" Susie groaned. "So close. I think I'll have a final drink to commiserate. Anyone else?"

Penny laughed.

"Any excuse for another drink, Susie."

"Of course. I don't get out much. Besides, my last one was lemonade, in case you didn't notice."

"I've still got some left, so not for me, thanks."

"Nor me," John said, downing the last of his Guinness.

"Okay, well, I've just seen my neighbour, so I'll walk home with her. I'll catch up with you later, Penny. Good night, John. See you next week if not before."

Outside, Penny stifled a yawn and realised how tired she was. Even though her working week finished on a Thursday, it had felt longer for some reason. She felt herself automatically draw closer to John as they walked in step, ambling through the quiet village towards her cottage.

Cherrytree Downs was always beautiful, in all seasons and all weathers, but particularly on a warm summer's evening in good company.

With the cottage only moments away, Fischer pulled towards the village green.

"Do you mind if we let Fischer run for a moment?"

John smiled and shook his head.

"Not at all. It's the least we can do for the little chap, considering he's waited so patiently in the pub for us to finish."

As they stepped onto the village green, Penny caught the scent of newly mowed grass. It was the one smell she instinctively associated with summer. She turned to John at the same time he turned to her. He took a step forward, and Penny held her breath. Then he sneezed. He pulled out a handkerchief.

"Cursed hay fever," he said. Wiping his eyes. The moment, along with what could have transpired, was lost.

"What happened to the handkerchief Fischer found in the hedge?" Penny asked. "Did you learn anything from it?"

"Some, but it wasn't immediately helpful. There's DNA on it as you'd expect, but without a match to someone in the database, all we can do is keep hold of it until we've got a person to link it to. The monogram was interesting. It could have been Alan Dubois, and he was a person of interest to start with, as you know, but we've ruled him out now. He might be an excellent bowman, but not even he could have shot Cotton from that distance with those bows. Whoever killed Derek must have been right behind him. Sorry, hang on, Penny," he added as his phone rang.

"Monroe," he answered. "You've arrested her? Yes, I see. All right, I'm on my way." He hung up and turned to Penny. "Sorry, I have to go."

"You've made an arrest?"

"Yes."

"Can you tell me who?"

John sighed and rubbed his hand over his face.

"I expect it will be common knowledge before long, but keep it to yourself, anyway. It's Janet Cotton. She's been searching on-line for whether life insurance will pay out if the insured was murdered."

"Well, that doesn't seem strange. I'd want to know too if my husband had been murdered."

"On the face of it, I'd agree with you, but she did this just hours before his death."

Penny gasped.

"Before? I see. Well, that does change things. I talked to her when she was collecting her stuff from the fair ground. She wanted a divorce, but Derek couldn't afford to give her half of the restaurant. It would have meant him losing it completely. There was no love lost between them, John. In fact, she seemed to be glad he was dead, but I honestly can't see her killing him."

"She has motive and opportunity, Penny. She went missing from the fair shortly before it happened. Put together with this added information, and she looks highly suspicious. I'll walk you back home before I head back to the station."

Penny smiled. She could practically see her cottage from where they were standing.

"It's fine. It will take me a couple of minutes to get home. You go and do your job."

"No, I insist."

Penny called to Fischer, who came bounding up exuberantly, then fell into step alongside Monroe. They were only a few feet from her front gate when his mobile rang again. He resisted the urge to answer it, but Penny could see he wanted to.

"It's fine. I'm home now. You should go."

Monroe nodded.

"I'll see you soon," he said, but to Penny, it almost sounded like a question.

"Next Thursday, if not before," she said, and stepped through her gate. She turned to close the latch, watching John, phone glued to his ear, jog back to his car which he'd parked at the pub. She couldn't help but wonder what would have happened if his phone hadn't have rung.

Then she thought about the reason for the call. Had Janet Cotton really murdered her husband?

TWELVE

"What do you want to do today then, Fischer?" Penny asked her little dog once breakfast was over and she was washed and changed.

In reply, he dashed to the hall and trotted back with his lead in his mouth, tail wagging so fast it was a blur. Penny laughed.

"Clever boy. Sugar hill it is."

The village was alive with people on their way to work when Penny and Fischer stepped through their front door. She saw Susie drive by on her way to the Gazette offices in Winstoke and waved. A couple of beeps on the horn told Penny her friend had seen her, too.

Ten minutes later, she was leaving the outskirts of the village and entering the fields. It was quiet and peaceful and as strikingly beautiful as ever. Penny took a deep breath and felt the stress leave her body as she exhaled.

Somewhere in the distance, she could hear the lowing of cows as they were moved indoors for milking. A low rumble of yet another tractor, barely audible, disappeared and was replaced by a sound Penny hadn't heard for a long time. She stopped and listened with Fischer at her heel. It was a Skylark, its notes descending to a silvery tinkle. Penny grinned, feeling her spirits rise.

"I must remember to tell dad and Mr Kelly about this, Fischer. The Skylark is once again nesting in Hampsworthy Downs."

A light breeze over the morning dew lingering on the grass, kept the summer's day under the bright blue sky pleasantly cool. She'd worn jeans and a long-sleeved lightweight shirt, but had packed a fold away anorak in her bag in case of a shower. Her walking boots had seen better days, but over the years had comfortably moulded themselves to her feet so much they were like slippers. Besides, they still had a fair few miles left in them.

As the morning warmed up, the breeze brought with it the scent of summer fruits from the pick-your-own farm. Penny had many fond memories of picking strawberries and raspberries with her parents. The rows of plump, ripe fruits filled with juicy sweetness proved too much to resist for her as a little girl, and she always left with great splatters of red down whatever she was wearing and a mouth like a clown.

Walking around the shoulder of sugar hill Penny glimpsed the village of Rowan Downs and the country road leading away to Winstoke. She turned and headed up the path to the top, Fischer bounding on a head full of beans. The views were breathtaking, encompassing a three hundred and sixty degree vista of practically the entire county, and she needed to see it today. She shifted her bag across her shoulder and started up the beaten earth track, the breeze building to a bracing wind the higher she climbed.

The path wasn't terribly steep, but climbed steadily upward. Fischer burst into a run as he spotted the flash of a white tail in amongst the ferns at the side of the path. In was in Fischer's nature to chase anything that moved, and she knew he wouldn't hurt the creature. He just wanted to play. But by the same token, rabbits were easily frightened, so she whistled and called him back. He sped towards her, tongue lolling and eyes sparkling as he enjoyed the freedom. She gave him a treat as a reward for his excellent recall, and several minutes later, they made it to the top of the hill together.

Penny stood for a moment, catching her breath while her little dog lay down beside her. She gazed around admiring the stunning views of the countryside. From this vantage point she could see Chiddingborne away to the north, Cherrytree Downs down below and even made out the patterns of the roads around her cottage. Far in the West, a few miles away, was the town of Winstoke. The main market street in the middle was wide and clear and she could see the silhouette of the old castle ruin standing proudly over the town.

She sat on a rocky outcrop and poured herself a cup of tea from the flask she'd brought, along with a bowl of water for

Fischer, who lapped it up gratefully. She'd just taken her first welcome sip when her phone rang. It was Susie.

"Penny. I hope I'm not disturbing you on your day off?"

Penny gazed over at the town, knowing Susie was down there at the Gazette offices.

"No, of course not. I'm sitting on the top of Sugar Hill with Fischer, having a cup of tea. Is everything all right?"

"Actually, I could kick myself for not remembering this before. It's because I didn't cover the story myself that none of the details really stuck."

"Susie, what is it?"

"I've been digging a bit more into Derek Cotton's background. There was a fatality at his restaurant. Ages ago now."

Penny halted her cup midway to her mouth as she tried to recall the incident.

"Oh my gosh, I remember it now. Food poisoning wasn't it? Something to do with a contaminated cooking pot?"

Penny could hear Susie shuffling papers at the other end of the line.

"That's right. The investigation found no evidence of unsafe or unhygienic practice. Apparently, a cooking pot had transferred minute traces of peanut oil even after being thoroughly washed. The Food Standards Agency ultimately determined it was a rare, unpredictable and tragic accident."

"How awful. I bet the chef was a nervous wreck trying to cook after that."

"Quite possibly. The old Scottish chef who worked there part time was off for the day. It was actually Derek Cotton who was in the kitchen cooking."

"I remember the Scottish chef. He was only about five feet tall and his hat was almost as high as he was. So, Derek was cooking when it happened? Who would have thought such a tiny trace of nut oil could cause such a severe reaction that someone could die from it? I tell you, Susie, I don't think I would dare eat out if I had such critical allergies."

"I know, it's a scary thought, isn't it? But do you remember who the victim was, Penny?"

Penny wracked her brains but couldn't.

"It was Mary Deacon," Susie said. "Tony Deacon's wife. She died on the way to the hospital that same night."

"Oh, that's right. It seems so long ago. Poor Tony."

"She used to hen peck him a bit, do you remember? But he never seemed to mind. She was always calling out Ant'nee, Ant'nee, with only two syllables... Hello? Penny, are you still there?"

"Oh, Susie, don't you see what this means? Everyone called him Tony, except his wife. He even introduced himself as Tony. That white handkerchief Fischer found in the hedge could have come from his pocket. It's the sort of gift Mary would have given him. A. D. Must be Anthony Deacon."

There was a prolonged silence on the other end of the phone.

"Susie? Don't you agree?"

"I think you're probably right about the hankie being his. There can't be many people with those initials around here, and we've already ruled out Alan Dubois. But, and this is assuming it's not one of the crowd of tourists who lost it at the fair, Tony could easily have dropped it elsewhere, miles away from where Derek was found, and it just blew into the hedge. And do you honestly think he could have shot Cotton with a bow and arrow? I don't think he could. Billy wanted a go and Tony only just hit the furthest target when he was demonstrating how to do it. Derek was standing way beyond that. Honestly, Penny, I don't think Tony has the skill necessary, and those bows are only made to go so far."

"But he has the best motive in the world, Susie. Revenge. And he has a bit of a temper, so I've heard."

"Yes, but none of that is proof, Penny."

Penny sighed.

"No, I know. But I think I'll pay him a visit, anyway. He has that small bungalow just outside Holts End."

"And what's he going to think about you just turning up at his door?"

"I'll tell him I was just passing on my walk with Fischer and wondered how he was getting on with the book he borrowed."

"Right," Susie said, in tones that suggested she thought Penny's idea was far from convincing. "Look, just promise me you'll be careful, will you? If you're right and Tony did kill Derek, you're walking into the lion's den. You've no idea how he'll react."

"He doesn't know I know, though, does he? Besides, I'll have Fish Face with me, I'll be fine. Anyway, you know where I'm going. If you don't hear from me by tonight, send the cavalry."

"Oh, just charming, Penny Finch. I'll be stuck in the office for the rest of the day worrying you've been knocked over the head and buried in the woods."

Penny laughed.

"It won't come to that. I'll be fine, Susie, don't worry."

Penny ended the call and put her phone back in her bag. As she did so, her hand touched on something unfamiliar. It was soft and squishy. Gingerly, she pulled it out. It was the piece of carrot cake she'd bought from Linda Green. The low fat, no sugar recipe.

"I suppose you don't need sugar to make a cake, do you, Fish face?" Then a thought hit her like a lightning bolt. "Do you need a bow to kill with an arrow?"

Penny stuffed everything back into her back and jumped up. Setting off at a brisk pace with her little dog scampering alongside. Her destination, Tony Deacon's house at Holts End.

THIRTEEN

Penny walked down the east side of Sugar hill, across the field and through Cringle Wood. She skirted the north bank of Freshwater Lake and out onto the country road that led into Holts End.

"I know how he did it, Fischer," Penny said as they strode over the field. "He must have seen the vet's receptionist leave the food marquee for the dog show, and then Dubois and Green exit. He must have realised Derek Cotton was alone. He could see all the comings and goings at the food marquee from where he was stationed at the archery range.

"He went to the end of the range and picked up one of the arrows. He crawled through that gap in the hay bale wall we discovered, you know, the part that hadn't turned yellow. Then crawled through the hedge and ran round to the food marquee from the road, going back through the hedge at that side. He wouldn't have noticed Jack Stone parked back up the road on the phone. If he had, he would have stopped.

"He got in the side of the marquee under the canvas right behind Derek Cotton. Alan and Linda were on the other side so wouldn't have seen or heard him. He must have been really quiet for Derek not to have realised he was there. But then again, there was a lot of noise outside and Derek was angry, his mind on other things. Tony then stabbed Derek in the neck with the arrow and reversed his journey back to the archery range. Jack Stone had already driven off by then so didn't see him. Fingerprints would have been irrelevant as his were on all the bows and arrows, anyway.

"But the blow wasn't instantly fatal, Fischer. Derek staggered out of the tent, looking for help, then collapsed. Maybe if we'd found him sooner, he would still be alive."

Fischer looked up at her and gave a little whine.

"I know, Fish Face, I'm sorry that wasn't fair. It wasn't our fault. You found him as fast as you could and raised the alarm."

She bent down and gave him a hug, scratching his neck.

"Come on, little man, we're almost there."

Just on the edge of the village, Penny found the overgrown gravel track road that led up to Deacon's bungalow. The painted sign at the edge of the road declaring 'Deacon Cottage' was weather-beaten. The paint chipping off and the wood rotten, so the words were barely discernible.

The short track was also in terrible disrepair. The path, once a neat tar covered crushed rock foundation, was now eroded, leaving deep ruts and pot holes. Wild Rowan trees on either side further constricted the narrow thoroughfare and Penny had to brush aside stray branches as she moved forward. Her shirt becoming snagged on more than one occasion.

Once past the trees, she arrived at a small overgrown garden. The last vestiges of what had clearly been at one time neat front lawn surrounded by flower beds, was now a tangle of weeds and wild grasses with a beaten path to the front door. She attempted to lift the moldy brass door knocker, but it was practically welded in place with dirt and neglect. She rapped loudly with her knuckles instead. After several hard knocks, which resulted in no answer, she took a step back.

Either side of the door, with its pale blue paint flaking leaving bare wood beneath, were small timber framed windows. Penny approached the right one, and cupping her hands around her eyes, tried to see inside. But with the amount of grime caking both the inside and the outside of the glass, it was impossible to make out anything.

To the left was what she assumed to be the kitchen window. Picking her way through the overgrown mint and lavender in the herb bed below, she peered through the glass. A shade cleaner than its counterpart, she could see what must have once been a very pretty little kitchen. Now it was an absolute tip. Dirty dished were stacked haphazardly next to a sink that was piled high with filthy pots and pans. A tap dripped into a saucepan that was already overflowing with dirty, greasy water. A pine table was piled with paperwork, fish and chip wrappers, an open ketchup bottle, and a tub of margarine with a knife sticking up out of it. There were several flies feasting on the contents.

Penny stepped back. The whole sight was making her feel sick. How could anyone stay healthy living in such an abominable state? She felt dreadful for Tony Deacon. He obviously wasn't coping at all well and was badly in need of help.

She moved round the house to the next window. It was a small living room, in the same state of severe neglect as the kitchen. Piles of laundry were scattered in various piles and draped over the furniture. Whether clean or dirty, or a combination of the two, Penny couldn't tell. More papers and lord knew what else covered every available surface. There was a path through mountains of debris between the door to a hallway and a single, empty armchair. In front of the chair was an old fashioned television set, with an aerial sat on top. Flickering static was on the screen. Penny was amazed the set was still working. She'd had one just like it as a student.

"Well, the TV is on," Penny mumbled to Fischer, who was sniffing along the pathways and digging in the flowerbeds. "Come on, don't dig, Fischer. We don't know what's under all that. I don't want you cutting your paws on glass or broken pottery."

Fischer trotted with her as she went to examine the last window. It was the bedroom. In complete contrast to the rest of the house, it was absolutely pristine. A clean bedspread lay over a double bed, with a polished brass bedstead. An open wardrobe door showed a neat arrangement of women's clothing and shoes. On the dark timber floor lay a brightly coloured rug, and on the dressing table, with its large oval mirror, a neat arrangement of bottles and tubs was displayed.

On a bedside table, Penny could clearly see a framed wedding photo. A grinning Anthony Deacon alongside his new wife Mary, smiling out into an unknown future.

Penny looked away, feeling guilty for having intruded on such a private and deeply sad scene. This single perfect room in a house of utter chaos and neglect was a shrine to a once happy and loving relationship and a love lost.

At the back of the house where overgrown brambles had taken over, Penny found a lean-to which created a porch like area surrounding the back door. Again, this area was a complete shambles. It housed an old rusty chest freezer, a washing machine in a similar state and a pair of rusted bicycles chained together, all nestling in a sea of old newspapers, clothes and assorted junk. Penny picked her way across the chipped and cracked linoleum floor to the back door. It was ajar.

She cautiously pushed it open and peered around the gap. Hidden from view of the windows, she found Tony Deacon lying on the floor. She rushed forward just as he moaned and curled in a fetal position, his arms clutching his stomach as he writhed in obvious agony.

"Tony, what's wrong?" Penny cried, scrabbling for her phone to call 999.

"Leave," Deacon gasped out.

His face was pale, waxy and sweating, his eyes were bloodshot, and his nose was bleeding.

"What's happened?"

But Tony didn't answer. It was then that Penny saw the open bottle of rat poison.

———•———

"Oh, Tony, what have you done?"

She relayed to the emergency operator that she needed an ambulance urgently for a man who had poisoned himself.

"No ambulance," Tony gasped. "Just leave me alone."

"I can't do that, Tony," Penny said, trying to fight back tears.

She'd had some first aid training and was frantically trying to remember what to do that wouldn't make the situation any worse. Water, that was it. She scrambled up and ran to the kitchen. Thankfully Fischer was still sitting in the doorway. She didn't want him anywhere near the rat poison.

"Good boy, Fischer. Stay there."

She grabbed the nearest cup and swilled it out quickly, then filled it from the tap. She ran back to Tony and, kneeling down, gently lifted his head and tipped the mug to his lips.

"Please, Tony, you need this water."

But he refused, clamping his mouth shut and turning his head away.

"Why, Tony? Why didn't you ask someone for help?"

"Who can help?" he rasped. "No one can bring Mary back. Just leave me to die."

"Did you kill Derek Cotton?"

"He deserved to die. He killed my Mary and got away with it."

He suddenly started to cough and retch and among the vomit, Penny saw blood. She grabbed the nearest thing to hand, a discarded sweatshirt, and wiped away the mess from his nose and mouth. She maneuvered him into a recovery position and held his hand.

"I'm nothing without Mary," he said so quietly Penny could hardly hear him. "Cotton got away with murder and now, so will I. But, I'll be with my wife and that's all that matters. It's all I want. To be with Mary again."

His eyes closed, and he lapsed into silence. Penny checked for a pulse and eventually found one, but it was faint. Tony Deacon was fading fast.

"Come on, stay with me, Tony," she said, praying silently for the ambulance to come quickly. But they were in the middle of nowhere and the ambulance was coming all the way from Winstoke.

She then called the only person she wanted to speak to, one who would be a source of comfort and support as she sat alone with a dying man, unable to help. It rang a couple of times, then switched to voice mail.

"John, it's Penny. I'm with Tony Deacon at his house. He's taken an overdose of rat poison. I've called an ambulance, but I don't think they're going to get here on time. He's admitted to killing Derek Cotton. He's unconscious. I can't help him,

John." Her voice caught, and she swallowed the sob rising in her throat. "Please, call me as soon as you can."

———•———

It couldn't have been more than fifteen minutes later when she finally heard the sound of the siren outside the bungalow, but it seemed like a lifetime to Penny as she held the hand of a man who was dying before her eyes.

She rushed to the front door just as the paramedics jumped out and led them to where Tony's inert form lay among the debris of his once pristine and happy life.

She returned to Fischer and the two of them walked round the side of the house and waited in the front garden while the paramedics did their work. Then her phone rang. It was John.

"Penny, I've just got your message. Are you all right? Are you still at Deacon's house?"

"Yes, I'm still here. The ambulance has arrived and they're working on him now. It doesn't look good, John."

"I'm just getting in my car. Stay there. I'll be with you as soon as I can."

Penny staggered to a nearby bench. The varnished had long since stripped away and the ironwork was rusty, but it was sturdy enough to take her weight. She slumped down, her knees finally giving way after the long walk and the shock of finding Tony Deacon. Fischer jumped up beside her and lay down with his head on her knee, eyes alert as he watched the door to the bungalow. She stroked his back, grateful for the contact of her best friend.

A moment later, the paramedics brought Deacon out of the house on a stretcher.

"Are you family? A friend?" one of them asked her.

It was an interesting question. She wasn't either. What sort of friend would let someone fall into the abyss like this? She shook her head.

"A neighbour."

"I'm afraid we can't let the dog into the ambulance," he told her as they loaded the stretcher into the back.

"It's all right. I'm waiting for DI Monroe. He's on his way over from Winstoke. I expect he'll come along to the hospital as soon as he can."

The paramedic nodded, then boarded the vehicle. It drove away, blue lights flashing and siren blaring as it charged back down the track, scattering gravel in its wake. It turned right onto the main road and sped away.

Ten minutes later, John Monroe pulled up and jumped out of the car. He must have really put his foot down to get there so quickly. Either that or he was nearer to Holts End than Penny had assumed. Bounding over, he enveloped her in a tight hug, much to Penny's surprise. She froze for a split second then leaned into his chest. Relief combined with exhaustion as the tears began to flow.

"I'm so sorry you had to witness this, Penny," John said into her hair. "I need to go and look around the house. Will you be all right here for a moment?"

Penny pulled away and wiped her eyes.

"I'll come with you. I'm okay, really. I didn't expect to find him like that. Do you think he'll make it?"

John shook his head.

"I honestly don't know. But you found him in time to give him a fighting chance. What made you come here?" he asked as they entered the house.

"You don't need sugar to make a cake."

He stopped and took her by the shoulders, turning her to face him.

"You're not making sense, Penny. You must be in shock. Please, go and sit in the car. I won't be long."

"I'm not. I'll explain later. What are you looking for?"

John sighed, but didn't argue. With Fischer sitting in the doorway, they ventured further into the bungalow.

"Dear god, what a mess," John said sadly, gazing at the squalor surrounding him. "Poor bloke. I was hoping he'd left a note, but it will be like looking for a needle in a haystack."

"There's one place it might be," Penny said, leading him to the immaculate bedroom. Propped against the pillow was an envelope. There was nothing written on the outside, but after donning a pair of latex gloves, John carefully extracted a letter. They read it together.

To whom it may concern,

This is both my confession and my last goodbye.

I have been more lonely than I can bear since I lost my beloved Mary and every day it gets worse. Derek Cotton murdered my wife, yet he got away with it. Why is he still walking around free when my wife is gone?

I was so angry at what he'd done I wanted revenge, so at the fair I sneaked out through the gap I'd left in the hay bale wall and went through the hedge. I went under the food marquee canvas at the side when I knew he was alone and stabbed him in the neck with an arrow. I then returned to the range the same way and saw him fall and die before anyone else noticed him.

But the relief at his death wasn't enough, and it didn't last. I didn't feel any better. In fact, I felt worse and Mary was still gone. Then I felt sorry for what I'd done.

Mary would have been so disappointed in me. I killed someone and I am more ashamed and guilty than I can describe here. I miss my beloved wife more than anything. I can't go on any longer.

May God forgive me for what I've done.
Anthony Deacon.

FOURTEEN

Penny slept fitfully that night, her dreams filled with the dying man in a mound of rubbish, who, in the way that dreams do, morphed into John Monroe. She woke up gasping and with fresh tears on her cheeks at the thought of losing John.

The way he'd held her in his arms at the bungalow yesterday had seemed like the most natural thing in the world. There was no awkwardness or discomfort. She just felt safe in his arms as though she'd finally found her place.

Fischer came bounding up from the foot of the bed and, with paws on her shoulders, began to lick away the salty tears with little whimpers of concern for his mistress.

Penny giggled at his antics and scooped him up, kissing his nose.

"I'm all right, Fischer. It was just a bad dream. Come on, let's go and get some breakfast."

An hour later, with Fischer playing in the back garden while Penny did much needed housework, it was time to go for a walk. She glanced at her watch and found it was still only a quarter to eight.

When she opened her door, there was a surprise on the step. A deep pink geranium in a pot shaped like a teapot. It was from Susie. Penny had sent her a quick text when she'd got back the evening before, explaining what had happened. Assuring her friend she was okay but didn't feel like company. Susie had immediately text back saying she understood and Penny knew where to find her if she wanted to talk. She must have dropped off this gift on her way home from work. Penny was surprised neither she nor Fischer had heard her.

"We'll put it on the table in the back garden when we come home, Fish Face," Penny said to the little dog, who was waiting patiently on the garden path with his lead in his mouth.

The village was quiet for a Saturday morning. At her parents' house, she saw the car was gone. No doubt they'd gone to town to do a shop at the supermarket and have lunch. Susie's car was parked in her drive, but all the curtains were drawn. Her best friend was enjoying a rare lie in.

Around the back of the village, she came across two boys walking together and chatting excitedly. They carried sticks that they wielded as swords one moment, then carried over the shoulders the next, marching like Buckingham Palace guards. They dived into the hedgerow at the edge of Cherrytree Downs and disappeared from view.

Coming around to the duck pond, Penny stopped by the green to let Fischer run across to his tree. But this time he kept moving and in the distance at the far end, she realised he was pelting towards a familiar face. Her heart gave a thump, it was John Monroe.

He gave her a grin and a wave as he lowered himself to greet the over excited dog, who was intent on giving his face a wash whether he needed one or not.

Penny laughed and jogged over, calling to Fischer to leave the poor man alone.

"Sorry," she said. "He's really pleased to see you."

"I can see that," John replied, standing up and wiping his face with a handkerchief. "And what about you?"

"Yes. I'm pleased to see you, too."

John took a step forward, and pulling her close, kissed her. Softly at first, then with more urgency. They pulled apart, both breathless.

"You've no idea how long I've been wanting to do that," John said.

Penny grinned.

"It was worth the wait," she said.

"So, how are you after yesterday?"

"Mixed emotions, actually. Glad I was there to help him, but sad and quite angry that he'd got into the state he had before anyone realised. I've always believed the downs are first and foremost a place of community spirit, where there is always someone to help you in a time of need."

"It is, but only if you ask for it, Penny. Tony Deacon was very careful to hide his true emotions and his suffering. If he'd have asked for help, then I know there would immediately have been half a dozen people who would have stepped forward. You included. You can't blame yourself."

"I know you're right, but I just feel as though we should have seen how badly he was doing. I should have asked him, John, not waited until he'd got so lost and desperate that he killed another person before attempting to take his own life."

"Oh, Penny," he said, pulling her in and holding her tight. "You're not a mind reader. You can only help someone if they really want it, and from what I've seen of Tony Deacon, he honestly didn't want anyone else knowing his business."

They pulled apart.

"How is he doing, John? Will he live?"

John took her hand, and they began to walk back along the green, watching Fischer running around following numerous scents.

"I honestly don't know. The doctors are doing everything they can, but he's in a bad way. If he does recover, then he'll spend the rest of his life in prison for murder."

Penny nodded.

"Pretty awful either way."

"Penny..."

"Uh oh, I have a feeling I'm about to get told off."

"I don't think you realise how much jeopardy you put yourself in yesterday. If you had any evidence Tony Deacon was the murderer, you should have called me and let us deal with it."

"I didn't know it was him. I had no evidence at all, just a hunch after I'd put a few things together."

"You and your hunches," Monroe said, trying to keep it light, but the concern in his eyes was palpable. "If you keep on with this amateur sleuthing of yours, you could find yourself in very real danger. I couldn't bear it if anything happened to you, Penny. Not now I've found you."

"It won't. Honestly, I'll be careful in the future. So you've obviously released Mrs Cotton, then?"

"Yes. We had no reason to hold her after Tony Deacon had confessed. Her search regarding life insurance payouts was purely coincidence."

Penny frowned.

"Do you really believe that?"

"It doesn't matter what I believe. We'll never know for sure her real reason or intentions, will we?"

They'd reached the end of the green and walked a little way up the road, before John stopped and looked at the house they were outside.

"The old police house," Penny said. "It's always been one of my favourite buildings. If it had been available and I'd had the money, I'd have got this instead of my cottage. It's always had such a homely feel to it."

"How would you feel about me becoming your neighbour?"

Penny grinned.

"Really?"

"Really. I put an offer in last week and it has been accepted. I should get the keys in the next couple of months."

"John, that's wonderful news."

He took a step toward her just as his phone rang. He swore with such feeling it made Penny laugh.

"Sorry, I've got to go."

"I know. Work."

He gave her a quick but passionate kiss, then set off jogging back to his car.

"Promise to stay out of trouble, Penny Finch," he called over his shoulder.

Penny turned and walked home with a ridiculous grin plastered on her face. She couldn't help it. Out of such an awful situation, something wonderful had happened, and she felt as light as air.

As she unlocked her front door, she wondered if John had noticed she hadn't actually promised to stay out of trouble.

If she'd had the power of hindsight, she would have known it was a good thing she hadn't, because less than two months later she was neck deep in another case, and this time she really was in trouble.

Finch & Fischer will return in **Driven to Death.** It's the Glorious 12th annual fundraiser at Thornehurst Grange, but among the confusion there's a tragedy and Penny and Fischer are once again caught in the middle. Coming in 2023.

Fancy a trip to 1930s England? Get your copy of **An Accidental Murder**. The first book in the series featuring Ella Bridges and her most unusual sidekick. Immerse yourself in country house murders, dastardly deeds at English Church fetes, daring escapades in the French Riviera and the secret tunnels under London, in the award-winning series readers call, 'Miss Marple meets The Ghost Whisperer.'

Available on Amazon, Waterstones and Barnes & Noble.

Have you met Lilly Tweed yet? Former Agony Aunt. Purveyor of Fine Teas. Accidental Sleuth? Get **Tea & Sympathy** now, the first book in the series and find out what happens when Lilly becomes the prime suspect in the death of a local woman.

Available on Amazon, Waterstones and Barnes & Noble.

You can stay up-to-date with new releases and sales by joining my Readers' Group. And get Ella Bridges' origin story; **The Yellow Cottage Mystery** as a thank you. Just go to the website for details: www.jnewwrites.com

If you enjoyed Fatality at the Fair, please do leave a review on the site where you purchased it. It doesn't have to be long, just what you liked about the book and who you think might like to read it. It really does help other mystery readers find the books.

Did you know The Tea Emporium, the shop in the Tea & Sympathy mysteries is now on-line? It's your ultimate resource for all things tea. From learning about the health benefits of Britain's favourite beverage to getting ideas and inspiration for themed events of your own. There's also help to find that perfect teapot, kettle or great gift ideas for the tea lover in your life. Visit **www.theteaemporiumonline.com**

ABOUT THE AUTHOR

J. New is the author of **The Yellow Cottage Vintage Mysteries**, traditional English whodunits with a twist, set in the 1930s. Known for their clever humor as well as the interesting slant on the traditional whodunit.

She also writes the **Finch & Fischer** and the **Tea & Sympathy** mysteries, both contemporary cozy crime series.

Jacquie was born in West Yorkshire, England. She studied art and design and after qualifying began work as an interior designer, moving onto fine art restoration and animal portraiture before making the decision to pursue her lifelong ambition to write. She now writes full time and lives with her partner of twenty-three years, along with an assortment of stray cats and dogs they have rescued.

Printed in Great Britain
by Amazon